# RHINO RITZ

*ALSO BY KEITH ABBOTT:*

PUTTY, Cranium Press / Blue Wind Press, 1971, poetry
RED LETTUCE (with Opal Nations), The Fault, 1974, poetry
12-SHOT, Z Press, 1975, photo/poem
GUSH: A COMIC NOVEL ABOUT UNEMPLOYMENT,
    Blue Wind Press, 1975, novel
THE BOOK OF RIMBAUD, New Rivers Press, 1976, prose/poems
WHAT YOU KNOW WITH NO NAME FOR IT,
    Cranium Press / Blue Wind Press, 1976, poetry
ERASE WORDS, Blue Wind Press, 1977, poetry
LOW-TECH BLUES, Forthcoming, novel

# KEITH ABBOTT

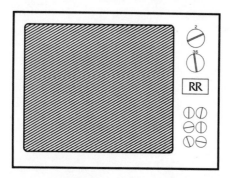

# RHINO RITZ
## An American Mystery

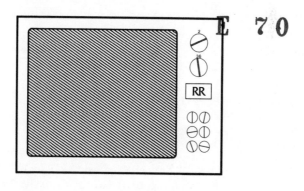

E 70

**Blue Wind Press  Berkeley 1979**

LIBRARY OF CONGRESS CATALOGING IN PUBLICATION DATA:

Abbott, Keith George, 1944–
Rhino Ritz: an American mystery with Ernest Hemingway, Gertrude Stein, Alice B. Toklas & F. Scott Fitzgerald.

I. Title.
PZ4.A1254Rh  [PS3551.B26]  813'.5'4  78-23542
ISBN 0-912652-42-X
ISBN 0-912652-43-8 pbk.
ISBN 0-912652-44-6 cloth signed & numbered 1-50.

Cover painting by Randall Snyder, Copyright 1979 by Blue Wind Press. Typeset by Lucy Farber. Designed by George Mattingly. Printed in the United States of America for Blue Wind Press, Box 7175, Berkeley, California 94707. First Edition, Spring 1979.

RR

*This book is for George Mattingly*

"It's an odd thing," said Oscar Wilde, "but anyone who disappears is said to be seen in San Francisco. It must be a delightful city and possess all the attractions of the next world."

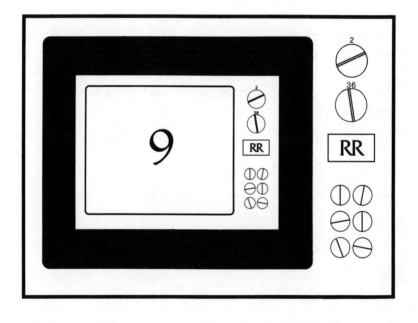

After the guests left, Gertrude Stein put her mandolin away
in the kitchen pantry. Alice was there, washing up.

—Did you have a good time, Pussy?

—Yes.

Gertrude looked at the mandolin in the pantry. Somehow the bank of wine glasses behind it was very attractive.

—I'm going to write some tonight.

—Very well.

—You're not sad?

—No.

—You seem sad.

—No, I'm not sad.

—But not happy.

—Yes.

Gertrude walked out of the kitchen and into the front
room. She jerked open the door leading to the hallway but
no one was there. Why did she think someone was there?
Only a short white shelf with a brown oak door at the end.
Then on the floor, Gertrude thought she saw a shadow coming under the door.

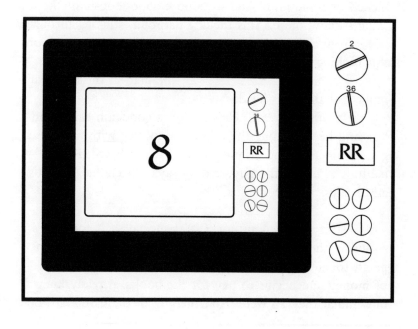

Meanwhile, in a bar on Clement Street. . . .

John Vaglia had a nose like a beagle and his eyes
drooped down in his sockets like marbles in flesh socks. The
inside of his mouth was redder than his lips: so much redder
that his lips looked preserved. He was drinking a beer and
talking to a man in a black suit beside him.

—Jesus, I tell ya.

— _____ , the man in the black suit replied.

—These guys. With money.

— _____ , the man in the black suit said.

—Jesus, I had this guy, well, I didn't even see him. I
was sitting there, I own the bookstore up the street, and
suddenly I hears this yell. Like someone's got their ankle
kicked or something. And woooooooooooooooooshhh! the next
thing I know there's this fucking harpoon, sticking through a
whole row of my books. The _whole_ fucking row! Stuck on
this fucking har _poon!_

— _____ , the man in the black suit
replied, shaking his head.

—It's this guy. . . . He's got on a goddamn cardboard
box and he's standing there in my doorway with this spear
gun in his hand and grinning at me. White beard. Kinda
balding. A big teethy guy, and he says: "Stendhal." That's
all he says. Just "Stendhal."

— _____ ?

—He's a French author. Got a special shelf for him.
Anyway, then in comes this other guy, a real shorty com-
pared to the clown in the box, and he pulls out a bunch
of money and begins to pay for the books. Already knew
how much they all were. And the guy in the cardboard box,

he stands there grinning until Shorty finishes paying and then they both lift up the whole impaled shelf of Stendhal and carry the fucking thing out of my store. They coulda killed somebody. I don't give a shit if that box guy is a famous author.

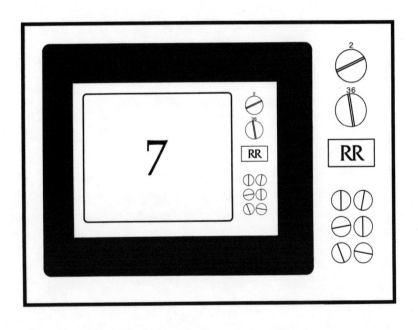

F. Scott Fitzgerald was trying to put his arm back on. It had fallen off in the street and he was trying to put it back on so he could drink some more. It was his right arm and he needed his right hand to drink with.

The Rue de Polk was dark and he was down on his hands and knees feeling around for his arm. Actually he wasn't sure that he'd lost it there. He couldn't remember exactly where or when he had last had a right arm.

Then he felt something wet under his left hand and he remembered that he was left-handed. Or he *thought* he was left-handed. The minute he thought it, it seemed true, and then he thought again and it didn't seem true. He wasn't all that sure.

He stood up unsteadily and tried to mop his chin, which felt wet. Had it been in the gutter too? He was surprised to find only a rough plaster-like chunk under his lips. Had he lost his chin too?

He decided to stop searching for himself and go on to Gertrude's. He was already late. She might be *short* with him.

At the corner of the Rue de Polk and L'Union, F. Scott Fitzgerald noticed a strange green glow around the streetlamp. Almost like absinthe. Absinthe. He hadn't had absinthe in years. The green glow grew deeper, greener. . . .

Just then someone moved off behind a car. A cab drove by. And it was raining, quite possibly raining. F. Scott Fitzgerald found himself lurching away from the huge bowl of absinthe on top of the pole. He stuck out his right hand and the cab pulled up beside him.

In the now white light of the street lamp he saw the

wet pinpricks of rain on the fingers and palm of his right hand. IT HAD COME BACK WHEN HE NEEDED IT!

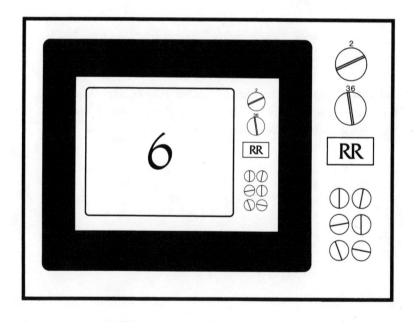

Gertrude was writing. She was writing very long and very short sentences. They mostly had the same words in them whether they were long or short. Except sometimes they didn't. Sometimes a strange new word would show up and then she would be delighted. Many of them were clear and many of them were clear for a long time.

    —You didn't get word from Scott?

    Without looking up. —No.

    —He's probably. . . .

    Alice bent over and touched the back of Gertrude's neck. It felt a little rough and a little soft. The folds rough but the skin soft. A strange feeling, both rough and soft.

    The pen . . . smooth in Gertrude's fingers. . . .

    —Goodnight.

    —Goodnight.

    As the door closed softly, Gertrude's mind stopped writing and she saw the shadow under the door again, but this time she saw the door open, and then a shelf of beautiful soft orange books. Her *Collected Works,* Random House. Gertrude wondered why she imagined that. As if opening that door would have given her her *Collected Works.*

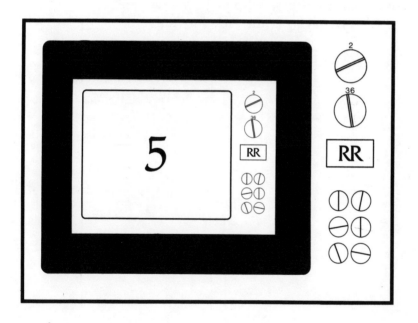

She had a short haircut, very black hair, and she was wet.

—This is the only cab for miles.

F. admired her as the cab lurched down the street.

—I just couldn't let you stand there in the rain.

She looked at him, drawing her white fur tighter around her neck. A line of rain hung on the window behind her and then slid off.

—We can stop for a drink and decide who gets the cab.

—What is your name?

—You speak good English. F.

—F.?

—That's right, F.

She smiled as she looked out the window. The black wet night going past. —Do you live near here?

—I'm staying at the Jack Tar Hotel.

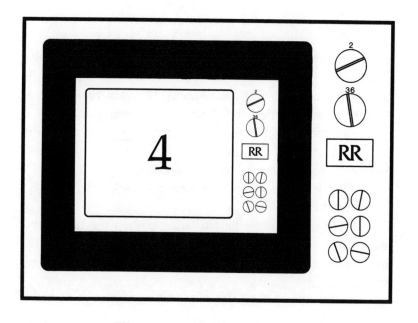

A soft chalk red, that's the color the 53 Chevy flatbed truck was painted. Smitty liked the way it looked. That's why he bought it. The oxidized paint gave it a misty quality.

Smitty was a little romantic about his truck, but why not? He'd put a big black bumper on the front, much larger than stock, and then he'd made the bed special, so Ernest could be strapped in back there standing up, just like they strapped in the daredevil wingwalkers in the air shows.

He pulled up in front of *Enrico's.* Ernie was in back, his guy wires taut, looking over the heads of all the people on the sidewalk. Smitty got out of the cab and climbed up to help unhook him.

—A good hunt.

—Right.

Smitty involuntarily looked down at the row of harpooned books in the front seat. He unhooked the wires from the brass clips on either side of Ernie's cardboard box. The box didn't look that sturdy, but Ernie had had it built special. Reinforced with *Duo-Flex X-17* nylon filament, 2,000 lbs. test. Ernie handed Smitty his spear gun and hopped nimbly off the flatbed. Even though he was wearing a box, Ernie could still move well, not as well as the years before he got packaged, but well enough.

—Put it in the garage and meet me back here.

—Right.

Ernie eased his cardboard bulk between the tables as the people either stared or pretended to ignore him. His table was in the corner; a special square chair, made for him, was behind it.

In the square chair, his edges fit comfortably. It had a

swivel-action that enabled him to take in all of nighttime Broadway. He grinned as a snifter of brandy was placed in front of him.

—Thank you, Jose.

When Ernest looked up, he saw a strange thing. There was a man standing next to the far wall . . . or at least it *looked* like a man . . . but his image was flipping up . . . slipping: the way a film slips in a projector. He was dressed as if for a safari, or it looked like he was. Ernest couldn't be sure because the next thing he knew the man was gone.

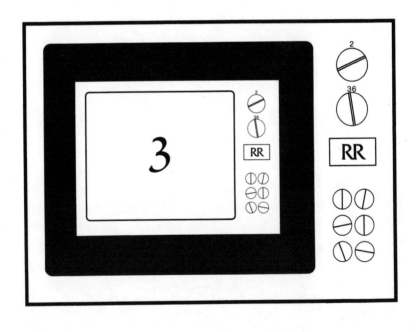

The hotel bed was damp. The white fur was also damp, but it made no difference as it lay across the damp sheets. F. Scott watched as the girl whirled around the room. Her white satin evening gown unravelled slowly from her body.

—I feel pretty, feel so pretty, so pretty, witty and wild. . . .

F. Scott answered the door. A split of champagne, some brandy, and the morning San Francisco Chronicle. $1.00 tip.

Brandy and champagne were poured together in the wide-mouthed plastic cup.

—What is it? she said into his ear as he lay on his stomach in bed, reading the paper.

He smiled at her. She giggled. He kissed her brow. It was hot. Then he kissed her eyebrow. Hairy. Then he kissed her nose and her lips and she kissed his nose and then his lips and forced her tongue into his mouth.

Satin running across the hand. Satin twisting across a thigh.

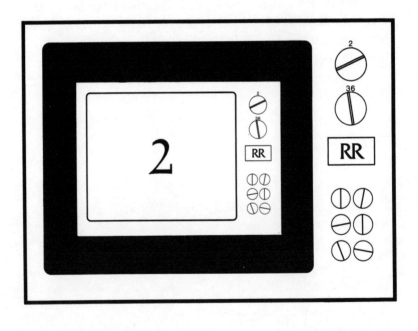

Gertrude went down the long white hallway turning off each light as she approached the bedroom. The doorknob was brass and cold and had a wonderful carved feel to it.

Alice was asleep. She lay in bed with the covers over one shoulder like a toga. Gertrude took off her clothes and put on a pair of flannel pajamas.

Then she lay down beside Alice. The rooftops out the window were still dark gray. Light was just turning the eastern sky a faint yellow.

Meanwhile, back in Gertrude's writing room, the pile of white sheets of paper was slowly dissolving into a light mist above Gertrude's desk.

CHAPTER TWO:

BYE-BYE SHERWOOD

Sherwood Anderson looked down on the early morning Rue de Budapest. A few of the shops were open, and the bars were being swept out. No whores were out; only Madame Christine was straggling up the street, her oversize bag in her hand. Sherwood wondered who she'd been with and where. She was a good old gal. A specialist, but still one of the locals.

Sherwood fondly remembered nights when they sat around the bar, singing "The Great Speckled Bird," "Tennessee Waltz," "D-I-V-O-R-C-E," and "Don't Come Home A-Drinkin' (With Lovin' On Your Mind)."

He'd had to explain the term "six-pack" to Madame Christine, who had thought it was some kind of appliance, like one of the many in her bag.

—No, he'd said a little sadly, —it's not one of those.

There was a strange windy sound from the room next door. Sherwood was worried about that. He'd been hearing that sound all night long. As if the wind were snaking through a steel pipe, a long steel pipe.

Like the sound of the prairie wind through a section of concrete drainage pipe.

Mlle. Wanda Love set the coffee and croissants down in front of the door to Room 13. She knocked. —Monsieur, voila! She smiled. That sounded perfect. Then she turned around and began to shuffle back down the stairs. —Oh darn, she said, —that was Sherwood's room.

Pulling up the hem of her short terrycloth robe with her right hand, she remounted the steps and knocked on the door again.

—Coffee and, Sherwood!

She started to leave again when she noticed that the door to the next room was slightly ajar. She stopped and then shrugged. Someone in the w.c. down the hall, probably.

As she stepped down the stairs, her hand automatically brought the thin red book out from the frayed pocket of her robe. She put one hand on the bannister and descended, her lips moving silently as she read.

—Voulez-vous. . . .

Just as she glanced down the list of objects you could want from room-service, she heard the sound of a tray being slid across the floor. When she was explaining things later, she said she never heard the door open and that the tray sounded like it was being slid down the *hall,* rather than into a room. But at the time, she hadn't thought about it at all.

Sherwood almost dug his toe into the mud before he remembered that he was still wearing his socks. Paris was too cold, especially in the fall, to go barefoot. But this! In Paris!

Sherwood slowly slipped one blue wool sock off his right foot and draped it over a cattail. Then he eased one toe into the clear green water. The ripples spread out from his toe in slow fat concentric waves.

The water was warm, almost lukewarm. . . .

Across the pond and over the stand of cattails, Sherwood could see the ruffled green pasture, a lone oak tree in the middle, and in the shade of the tree, four black-and-white patches that he knew were Holstein cows.

Sherwood looked back behind him at the partially open door, the tray in the doorway, the steam rising off the coffee. The paint was peeling off the door. A dull gray paint. The molding around the door was splintered. The wallpaper, some floral pattern long since faded into blotches of faint pink and green, was stained, ripped, and hanging.

It had something to do with the fifth floor but later Mlle. Wanda Love couldn't remember what had brought her up there. She might have just been doing one of the many things that needed doing in a hotel.

She saw the door to Sherwood's room open, so she stepped in to say hello. His room was empty. She looked down the hall and saw the door to the w.c. was open. Then she noticed the door next to Sherwood's was open, and she remembered the guy who had rented it.

She was going by it when she was startled to see a pair of blue socks in the middle of the room. For some reason she *knew* they were Sherwood's.

Wanda stepped up to the door and looked around the dingy room. A bed. A dresser. A chair. But something was wrong. The furniture was all pushed to the left side of the room, and the entire right side of the room was bare. Except for Sherwood's two blue wool socks.

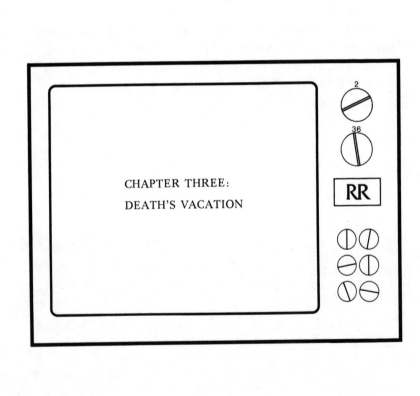

CHAPTER THREE:

DEATH'S VACATION

RR

—You don't want to mess with with acid, Ernest said, shaking his head, —you'll lose your point of view.

—I don't know, seems. . . . the earnest young man with the blue eyes started to say.

Ernie punched him in the shoulder. —Don't mess with it. You'll lose your point of view, and when you lose that, you've lost what you need. You may not think you need it. You may think that *any one* will do, but if you lose your point of view, you've lost everything. Past present and future will get all mushed up. P.O.V. is time. And acid gives you a vacation from it. A deadly vacation. You always need a *here*.

—Hunting good? the Marine broke in.

—Stendhal.

—The whole works?

—As much as was translated in the _____ edition.

Smitty smiled to himself as he looked out at Columbus Avenue and the park. He'd scouted out a new little bookstore down in the Mission and he was waiting for Ernie to see the 11th edition of the Encyclopedia Brittanica that he'd uncovered. Smitty wondered how he could get Ernie to take along the big gun without Ernie getting wind of the project. Maybe if he loused it up a little, said it needed . . . repairs. . . .

—Call for you, Mr. Hemingway.

The people around the table sat back a little as Ernie left for the back of the restaurant. It was the usual group of hangers-on that cluster around any famous writer. The guy with the blue eyes and earnest expression, the one with the red scar under his right ear, the Marine, and the four Japanese with tape recorders hidden in their large opaque sunglasses.

Ernie plucked at Smitty's sleeve when he returned.
—That was Gertrude. Trouble.

Smitty stood up and put on his coat. The people at the table shifted back in their chairs as Ernie grinned.
—Sherwood's missing.

Ernie and Smitty turned and went out the door. Everyone else at the table just sat there. Suddenly they were left with themselves. Fame had been a tiny dam in the stream of their mortality and now they felt the flow of the day take them up again and go meandering off into pointlessness. The Marine looked at the guy with the scar and the four Japanese each took the opportunity to adjust their sunglasses, each secretly flicking off the tape recorders hidden within. The young man with the blue eyes looked dejected.

The Marine yawned. Slowly he got up and nodded to the table. —Guess I'll mosey on, he said.

After they left their admirers at the Washington Square Bar & Grill, Ernie and Smitty got their flatbed out of hock at the Police Station garage and drove up Stockton Street as from in back Ernie shouted out the information to Smitty.

Smitty had had the back window taken out so he could talk to Ernie while Ernie was strapped in. It was colder that way, especially on those cold San Francisco evenings, but Smitty didn't mind. He wore a nice Duoflex X-17 Arctic parka.

—She says the concierge or whoever found Sherwood's room empty and his socks in the next room. Smitty grinned back at Ernie.

Ernie shook his head. —Naw, that's not it. Says some guy rented that room and one thing Sherwood's not is queer. He's nowhere usual. Checked all the usual flophouses, whorehouses and feedstores: he's not anywhere. Gertrude's worried. The place is on the Rue de Budapest, right by the Gare St. Lazare. . . .

Smitty nodded, mentally consulted the map of Paris, and found the quickest way there. He turned left on Geary and began to wind down the narrow streets of the city of Paris.

—We've come about Sherwood. Miss Stein sent us.

Mlle. Love put her little red book in the pocket of her housedress and opened the frosted glass door. Smitty stepped in first, then Ernest turned sideways and eased his bulk in through the narrow doorway. After introductions she led them up the stairs.

—I mean, when I took this job, I didn't know I was going to have to learn French.

—San Francisco's a bi-lingual city.

—Well, I've heard that Paris is the San Francisco of Europe, but I didn't know that half the people here can't even give you the time of day in English.

—Doesn't take long. Read the newspapers.

—This is it, fifth floor. He's got the room right there, at the head of the stairs. The door's open. Go on in. And the room next to it, that's open too. That's where I found his socks. You go ahead and look around. Are you friends of his?

—Yeah.

—I just don't know what happened to him. I talked to Madame Christine and she hasn't seen him either.

—Madame Christine?

—Huh? Oh she's the whore Sherwood's been palling around with. They go out and drink before she starts work. She's not really his type. She's got this ghastly red hair and she carries around this canvas bag. A *Fly United* bag. You can't miss her. Look around.

Ernie began to go through Sherwood's dresser. Smitty watched him for a moment and then he began talking.

—You know what I think, Ernie? He's got the guilties again.

—Think so?

—Yeah, and you know what he does then. Straight back to Iowa or Ohio. Anytime Sherwood starts palling around with a French whore he starts thinking about home again.

—That's not what I think about when I'm fooling a-round with a French whore, Ernie said, lifting a manuscript out from under a pile of underwear. He smiled over at Smitty. —Well, looky here, Sherwood's been doing a little chippy-ing on the side. Let's see. . . .

Smitty watched Ernie reading the manuscript, and then walked away. That was one thing that irritated Smitty, all this sneaky writing. He didn't know why they couldn't just be immortal and leave it at that. Besides, it was in the con-tract. It irritated Smitty, especially the way that Ernie pre-tended to be observing it all to the letter and was so sancti-monious about everyone else's transgressions. Smitty'd seen his pile of manuscripts shoved down there under the spare spear guns. And then all that stuff about *not coming around in the morning because I'm sleeping in* that Ernie gave him.

—Look at that, Ernie said, shaking his head, —another novel about a roofing contractor who wants to go off with the dark waitress down in the barrio and ends up wandering off into the night and leaving his wife instead.

Smitty didn't say anything, just poked around under Sherwood's bed. He drew out a pair of shoes.

—Well you may be right, about Sherwood going back to Iowa, Ernie said, throwing the manuscript on the bed, —but you know they haven't finished the bridge to Iowa yet, and he'd have to take the ferry across the bay, and Sherwood's scared silly of drowning. Loves ponds and creeks. But lakes, they're chancy: and bays, oceans? No way. Too dark and deep.

They went into the next room as Mlle. Wanda Love stood, memorizing irregular French verbs. Ernest looked down at the two blue socks on the floor. Then he walked back into the bedroom and came back out.

—Look at the way the furniture is all pushed to one side of the room.

Ernie and Smitty regarded the furniture. Then Ernie shook his head. —No, something's happened, Smitty. None of his shoes are missing and here's his socks. He wouldn't go out without his shoes and socks. No, something's happened to Sherwood, something bad.

Gertrude and Alice were holding hands when Hemingway and Smitty were admitted. The two women looked up and smiled at them. The maid brought out the *eau-de-vie* and served small glasses of it all around.

 —Well, Gertrude said, —what did you find out, Hemingway?

 —Nothing much. Sherwood's taken a powder.

 —You mean he's blown town, Alice put in.

 —Might be on the lam, Gertrude said.

 —Might. Then again somebody might have deep-sixed him.

 —Sleeping with the fishes, Smitty said softly, gazing up at the Cézanne above his head. It looked funny upside-down. Like the view through a periscope with delirium tremens, focusing on a plate of fruit.

 —What's the odds of him just being on vacation?

 —Are you kidding, Gertrude? Sherwood on vacation? There's no such thing as a vacation for Sherwood. Death'll be the only vacation Sherwood ever takes.

 —Maybe you guys could call this caper DEATH'S VACATION, Smitty said helpfully.

Gertrude and Hemingway stared at Smitty. Alice looked away in embarrassment.

 —Well, for one thing, we are not in a cheap detective novel. This is real Literary Life, Gertrude said concisely.

 —No, I am not joshing, Hemingway. What do you think has happened to him?

 —I don't know. But I think it's bad, whatever it is.

 —Kidnapped?

 —Maybe.

—By whom?

Ernest shrugged. At least it looked like a shrug. His box moved up and then down like a shrug.

—Who'd want a Classic American Author?

Gertrude and Alice sat there for a long time after Hemingway and Smitty left. (—It's funny, Alice had once said to Gertrude after Hemingway had been there, —but everytime he leaves, *it's as if the air were disturbed* and we have to wait for it to settle and clear.)

Gertrude turned to Alice and kissed her on the cheek. —Well, she said, —at least we know Sherwood's barefoot.

CHAPTER FOUR:

THE YELLOW CHAPTER

F. Scott Fitzgerald slowly ran his finger down his jaw. He was surprised. No mark at all. He turned his face the other way and stared at the mirror. Nothing there either.

He wiggled his ears. Perfect. What could have happened?

In the mirror he caught a glimpse of a white thigh leaning out from the doorway. The back of a head of red hair. Red hair?

F. Scott turned and walked out of the bathroom. The girl was just wriggling into a soft yellow velvet dress.

—Good morning.

—Good morning.

When F. Scott started to sit down on the bed the girl began giggling. —What's. . . ? he asked.

—You don't remember how I got here or who I am, do you?

—Nu-no, no. I must confess I don't.

She laughed. She was very pleased with herself. —I didn't tell you. You're very easy to distract. Every time you'd ask, I'd distract you.

—Well now, that's very interesting. How did you distract me?

—Easy. She began to wiggle one foot into a pale yellow high-heeled shoe. —You know you're just about perfect.

—I am? F. Scott Fitzgerald looked down at his knees. They seemed to be sticking out of his shorts at an odd angle. He let the right knee wobble a little and it felt okay, but. . . .

—You are one of the best lovers I've ever had. And you're just wonderful besides.

—Really?

—Yes you are. Has anybody ever told you that?

F. Scott nodded. —Everyone lately. I've been going to bed with one beautiful girl after another, night after night, and . . . I don't know if I should tell you this. . . .

—Go ahead.

He stopped. Watching her bend over, he saw the soft small ridges of her spine push up under the yellow velvet, and then her face looked back at him: perfect tipped small nose and the pleased, expensive expression of a child, a wild child.

—Well, what were you going to say?

—Uh, every night I think that I've lost parts of my body.

—You have a perfect body.

—I think my arm's fallen off, for example.

—It didn't. . . . Why do you stay in this hotel?

F. Scott looked vaguely around the room. He shrugged. —I don't know. Maybe staying in the Jack Tar Hotel is some kind of penance. If I stay here I notice that I don't get hangovers. I don't know. It just feels right.

—Welcome to Purgatory, she laughed. Her lips had a strange round shape with a little dimple in the middle of the upper lip; her finger came up to it and explored it hesitantly.

F. Scott watched her and felt a vague warm glow come to his head—the flash of kissing that dimple—the feeling of his tongue there—and she was watching her face in a mirror and he was watching her face there too.

The phone rang.

High above North Beach, in his wigwam on top of Coit Tower, Ernest was being asked questions by his Indian wife, Ku-na-so-way.

—Then how does one become a Local Author?

—It's tough. First of all you have to spend a lot of time Back East. Attend the right schools there and then spend a decade or so in publishing. Then you come out here and become a Local Author.

—Are there not many poets here?

—They are not Authors.

—But they live here and they write.

—That is correct, Ku-na-so-way. They live here and they write here but they are not Authors, so they can never become Local Authors.

Ku-na-so-way arranged the hem of her buckskin dress and resumed her slow scrubbing of the Balzac volume in front of her.

—But you can become an Unlocal Author. For that you must go to the right schools Back East and then publish with the small presses Back East and win fellowships and grants and such, and then come out here and live here and publish your books with the small presses out here but you are never reviewed and you must understand that you are an Unlocal Author, and therefore can't expect much.

Ernest followed Ku-na-so-way out the flap and into the wind howling around the wigwam. Strung around the guardrail was a white Duoflex X-17 monofiliament line with Vols. I-V of the *Collected Balzac* hung up to dry. As Ku-na-so-way clothespinned the sixth volume to the line, Ernest continued his story.

—Now if you are a writer born in this area and you don't go to school in the East and you don't become involved with publishing and you publish three or four books with the presses back there and maybe two or three books with the presses out here, you can expect to receive a notice when your worst book appears—say a book of travel diaries and short reviews that your publisher wants to market as a loss-leader—and then you may become a Local Author if you do not publish any more books for several years and perhaps die as your last book is published.

—But are not you and F. and Sherwood Local Authors? Ku-na-so-way shouted into the wind.

—No, we are dead, and that is even better than being a Local Author here in San Francisco. That way. . . .

Ernest turned to look at what Ku-na-so-way was looking at: he found F. Scott standing there, his white linen pants and coat flapping like a slack sail, his hand mashing his white linen hat down on his head.

—Jesus Christ, Hemingway, can't you live someplace else? There's a gale up here.

F. Scott Fitzgerald followed the wall around, inspecting
the perfectly stuffed and tanned books that were mounted
on it. A really amazing job had been done on them: you
could hardly tell where the harpoon had gone through, even
on the leather-bound volumes.

—She's some little taxidermist, isn't she? Ernie said,
nodding over at Ku-na-so-way as she fixed drinks.

—Marvelous. When'd you get the Twain? That's the
complete American Publishing Series, isn't it?

—Yeah. Smitty got wind of it over by the University,
so we dropped over there one afternoon when we knew the
guy was in. He wasn't in all that much, but we scouted a-
round and got the place cased, then went in and it went
fine. The first shot.

Ku-na-so-way handed Ernest his daiquiri and F. Scott
his Shirley Temple. Then she retired to a far corner and continued to scrub the Balzac.

—She's the only one who can fix a drink like that *and*
stuff a book. . . . But did you get any leads on Sherwood?

—No. No one's seen hide nor hair of him.

—I just don't like it. Sherwood's not going to leave
Paris just like that, especially not without his blue socks.

Ernest rubbed his cardboard box pensively. —Yeah,
those socks were knitted for him special by an old high
school teacher of his. When I checked with the whores on
the Rue de Budapest, all of them said he never took them
off.

—Any leads at all? Did he say anything? Been seeing
anyone regular?

—No one except this Madame Christine. She's appar-

ently a specialist, and no one's seen her lately. That's not odd: she sometimes gets long assignments, but still. . . .
    —It's suspicious, alright.
    —Where do you think we should start?
    Ernest appeared to shrug inside his box. —Don't know. But someone who was going to take off, say if Sherwood *did* take off. . . .
    —He's been known to do that.
    —Yeah, but I think there's more to it than that. If someone *were* going to make off with Sherwood, what would they do with him once they got him?

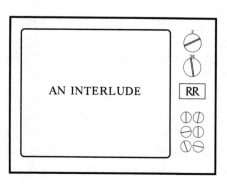

Sherwood tugged gently on the carrot top until the earth ruptured around it. It came up long and orange, with little white filaments of root waggling crazily with clods of dirt. . . .

—Little root-dirt pendulums, the carrot and the pendulum, no, the carrot and its pendulums: a collection of short garden stories. . . .

The rich dirt smell mingled with the carrot smell and the smell of crushed carrot greens. . . .

Sherwood was brushing the dirt off the roots when he saw the grooves spiraling around the outside of the carrot, where it had been machined.

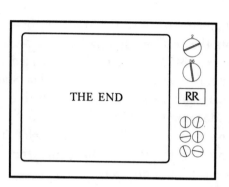

Gertrude climbed back into the Model T, first taking the mandolin off the seat and setting it in the back seat.

—They say this Madame Christine started working the street about three weeks ago. They say that Sherwood took a liking to her right away and they began to drink in the bars before Madame Christine went to work.

Alice nodded once and put the Model T in gear. They began bumping up the Rue de Budapest. One of the whores waved to them from a doorway.

—And she's not there now.

—No, Pussy, she's not.

—What did Sherwood and Madame Christine do together?

—Apparently they had a little friendship and then they just sat and drank and sang songs.

—Did any of them overhear anything?

—Well, this little *poule* back at the Cat's Garter said that Sherwood seemed to think Madame Christine reminded him of the old high school teacher who knitted his socks. Another one said that she reminded him of his home-town librarian. People said they cried a lot when they drank. At least Sherwood did.

—Should we go tell Hemingway what we found out?

—Certainly.

—Well, if that's all we have, we haven't much.

Ernest signalled the waiter for another round. He leaned back in his specially-built chair and grinned at Gertrude and Alice.

—Sherwood's probably in that line there, waiting to get into Finocchio's and see the drag show, he said, nodding toward the line outside of Enrico's.

F. Scott looked up from his iced tea at the line of maroon-pants-white-shoes-white-belts-&-chrome-glasses-guys with their dolled-up gals. He shook his head sadly.

—Now don't be depressed, Scott. You have your world and they have theirs, Gertrude said firmly, —and you stick to yours and you'll be all right. After all, Scott, Alice and I wouldn't be here if the Bank of America hadn't moved Paris into the financial district after France defaulted on their loan. They could have chipped it and moved it into their computer just like they did to the financial district. They didn't *have* to move it here.

—Yeah, maybe it was corporate conscience, but I think they did it so they could have their building next to the Eiffel Tower and cash in on the gawker's trade. Besides, *they* probably think their building looks better. Actually it looks like an amputee robot next to the Eiffel Tower.

—Oh Scott, it's much nicer this way. Now not only is there a there here but we can be both here and there here and that's better than no there anywhere but over there.

—*Over there, over there,* Ernest sang softly.

Alice and Gertrude sipped their Grand Marnier & Banana milk shakes (or *Le Grand Banane,* as Alice called it) with a giggle. Gertrude said she thought it should be called

*Le Grand Jaune,* but Alice poked her and told her she was no fun. Gertrude looked uncomfortable for a moment then gave a little wan grin and agreed to Alice's appellation.

F. Scott fiddled with his iced tea, and Ernest watched the crowd going by with his usual attentiveness, as Alice and Gertrude finished off *Le Grand Banane.*

—I think we ought to go over to the University of Iowa and scout around, Ernest said.

—I'd love to. We haven't been there in years, Alice said. She glanced at Gertrude for approval.

—Let's go in your car, Scott. It's big enough for all of us. . . .

—You mean it's big enough for *you,* Scott said, eyeing Ernest's box.

—What's the matter, you morose?

—No no, I just think this is a little bit bigger than you think.

—The car or . . . what do you mean?

—I don't know. I just think it.

—Scott, you do that so well, just thinking and not knowing. Don't ever change, Gertrude put in sweetly.

Scott signalled for the car, and the chauffeur brought the gleaming yellow 1936 Cord convertible around to the front of Enrico's. The chauffeur gave Scott the keys and then Scott fired him. It was a purely mechanical gesture.

—We get the rumble seat! Alice said gaily, climbing in back. Gertrude looked embarrassed and then pleased, and climbed in after Alice as Scott held the door open.

—You *guys,* he said.

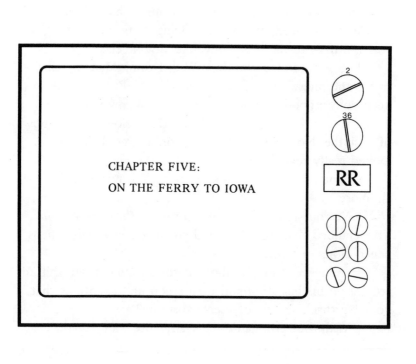

CHAPTER FIVE:

ON THE FERRY TO IOWA

2

36

RR

On the ferry to Iowa, F. Scott and Ernest went topside
while Gertrude and Alice stayed in the car.

—It's been years since I've been in a rumble seat! was
all Alice could say to them. Gertrude didn't seem to be interested in talking.

While Ernest and F. Scott were in the ferry bar waiting
for their drinks—Ernest agreeing that it was okay for F.
Scott to drink one drink while he was out of Gertrude's
sight—they discussed the case of the missing Sherwood.

—Why do you think he'll be over at Iowa?

—I don't know. It's a hunch I've got. Maybe if we talk
to one of the professors over there, he'll know of some con-
vention or something that Sherwood might have ducked off
to. He always needs the money. Being immortal is great, but
you still have to pay your bills like anyone else.

F. Scott nodded glumly. —Well, I think Madame Christine is the one we should go after, myself. But if it will
keep you in good humor. . . . Hey, you know what happened to me the other night? I had this vision. A huge bowl
of absinthe. No kidding. It was up on a street-light. It
looked really real.

—Scott, you were drunk. That stuff is not available
anymore.

—No, but it was real. I'm sure of it. I'm sure I could
have climbed that light-pole and got it if a cab hadn't happened along just then.

Hemingway thought about it for a moment. He shifted
around on his bar stool and then stood up. —Scott, is that
your big thrill, or one of them—absinthe?

—Yeah, but you can't get it anymore. . . .

—And when did that happen? The night Sherwood disappeared?

—Yeah, but. . . .

—About what time?

—In the morning, early morning.

Ernest's mind flashed back to the man he'd seen while he sat at Enrico's. Not quite real: like a man cut up by a bad splice in a film. —But it was real? I mean, the absinthe?

—As real as I'd want it to be. Why?

—I think we better go talk to Gertrude.

—She says that something funny happened to her that night too. Or that morning. She said that she was sure someone was outside her door. But she didn't know who. She said she too had this very strong hallucination.

    —What was that?

    —She didn't want to tell me at first. Finally she said it was *The Collected Gertrude Stein* by Random House. She said she thought that if she opened the door *The Collected Gertrude Stein* would be there. Even had the binding just the way she always wanted them.

    —How was that?

    —Orange.

There was a flat hard-sounding *flup* as the wind hit Ernest's cardboard, flexing it in and out. The ferry hit one side of the landing with a hollow creaking crunch, then it swung ponderously back to bash the other side. Ernest and F. Scott turned and went back to the Cord.

    —I've always liked ferry landings for some reason, Ernest said.

CHAPTER SIX:

THE TEMPTATION
OF ERNEST HEMINGWAY

The University of Iowa at Berkeley is a large, spacious campus with rolling, well-kept lawns and many botanical wonders. The Campanile overlooks the entire town of Berkeley and the farmlands beyond. To the south of the campus lies Telegraph Avenue, so-named in honor of the first form of mass communication to arrive in Iowa, because communication is the first task of any great University. Here, at the U. of I., the visitor can find many of the students working their way through the University by selling their agricultural products in picturesque street stalls. The atmosphere of a state fair is ever-present.

Primarily known as an "Ag" school, the University also boasts a growing liberal arts faculty, and a keen desire among its academic members to broaden the scope of its educational mission.

Especially famous are the schools of animal husbandry. Here the shoats of today become the pigs of tomorrow. And special care is lavished on the sows. For many years the University of Iowa at Berkeley has been known for the developmental matrixes which eventually led to the refinement of the super-hybrid female porker, so that now the "wombpork" is a brand name for a sow whose womb area accounts for over 45% of her body weight. Now, of course, these practices are universal but their beginnings are as surely rooted urp xerzzzzzzzzzzz gurk. . . .

—Is that why they're all wearing galoshes and coveralls? Alice asked, putting the tiny tape recorder back down on the seat between F. Scott and Ernest, (To herself: —Remember to give that back to the guard at the gate when we go out.)

—Yeah, I think so.

—What about *those* types?

—Those guys in jackets and military caps? Ikies. Big hero for them is Ike. Easy enough to get the gear.

—Was he really what they say? Alice put in.

—A trans-sexual? Don't know really. The Ikies get angry if you bring it up. But there's those rumors of the vitagene change with that clone of his, what's his name?

—Dick.

—Right. And apparently Mamie got mixed up with the thing, stumbled into the oval cloning chamber at the wrong moment and one of them ended up with a. . . .

There was a silence and then Gertrude cleared her throat.

—Poor Mamie, Alice put in.

—But they still idolize him here in Berkeley, Gertrude said.

—Right. And they invoke Presidential Privilege whenever there's talk of digging any of the principals up and having a look-see.

—There's the American Literature Department, F. Scott put in, steering the Cord onto a dirt road. At the end of the road was a quonset hut. It had been painted a dark blue, but the paint was flaking off, and now it looked like half a drainage pipe poking up out of the yellow clay dirt. Surrounding it were peeling eucalyptus trees, bark and leaves littering the ground around the hut.

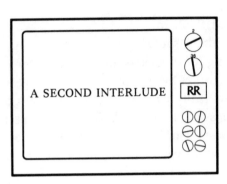

A SECOND INTERLUDE

Sherwood Anderson was pounding on the plastic walls and screaming.

 —I want out of here! Where's my hotel room? I need a drink! I don't want to be here! Fuck Iowa! Lemme out! I want out of here! Who the fuck *are* you? Let me out of here!

 Kick. Pound. Slap.

 —Fuck Iowa! I want out of here!

 Outside the clear plastic one-way walls two Japanese gentlemen were addressing each other.

 —Notice colloquial language, one said.

 —Yes. Like talking. the other said.

 —Yes, talking. But not real talking.

 —Talking like a book talks, but better.

 —Not book talk but people talk. Better than people talk.

 —Yes, the other said.

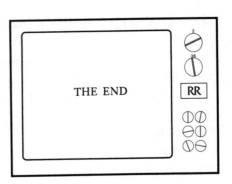

—Pretty shabby, F. Scott said, looking around the ceiling of the quonset hut. —Must be temporary.

—Temporary my ass, Ernest said, —this is a dump— whether it is temporary, permanent, or just a dream.

Alice tapped the desk. A secretary was asleep in a chair behind it.

She opened one eye. —Yeah?

—We'd like to see the chairman.

—Is it important?

—Why don't you let *him* decide.

—What if he's not here? she said yawning and stretching.

—Then we will hunt him down no matter where, and kill him, F. Scott said amiably. He smiled at her.

—Who shall I say is calling?

F. Scott watched as she picked up the phone. After punching a red button, she looked up expectantly. —Say it is F. Scott Fitzgerald come to pay his respects and ask a few questions.

The secretary dialed a number. —Yeah, there's a guy to see you here. Says his name is F. Scott Fitzgerald. Um. Okay. Yeah, sure. No, not yet. I'll get right on it. Right.

She put down the phone.

—You can go in. It's down at that end of the hut. She pointed at the door in the wall to her right. There was nothing on the door to indicate there was anything behind it. For a moment Ernest imagined that it led back outside.

Gertrude walked over and opened it. She looked back at the others. —Are you coming or not?

—Jesus, I don't know if I can get in there, Ernest said, turning sideways so his box could slip through the narrow door to the Chairman's office. —This is worse than getting into the nose of a B-26.

F. Scott, Gertrude, and Alice turned back toward the Chairman as Ernest eased into the tiny room. The Chairman was sitting behind a desk piled high with dusty mounds of paper. The shoulders of his suit were speckled with dandruff, and above his thick dark glasses, hair sat on his head like a pile of disturbed string.

—Ah, yes, he said, nodding toward Ernest dimly, as if he were at the other end of a *much* larger room, —I've read a great deal about you.

—But, he continued, squinting up at F. Scott, —how can I help you?

F. Scott told him.

—Oh my goodness, he said, sudddenly seeing a pile of papers under a thick layer of dust and taking the pile to scrape the dust off into a wastebasket beside the desk. —You must be mistaken. Where would we get the money, and why on earth would we give it to . . . a writer, if we had it? No, I haven't seen him, though you could check with my secretary and she might be able to help you.

—You do know who Sherwood Anderson is, don't you?

The Chairman peered over the paper on his desk at Ernest. —Yes, of course, but we don't have that kind of money anymore. We hardly have any money for our teaching assistants, and of course the graduate studies has been severely cut . . . I guess I'm really not much. . . .

—You do have a course on him, don't you?

—And Gertrude, Alice put in. —You also have one on Gertrude, don't you?

The Chairman shrugged. —Actually no, we don't. He looked up at them in a distant, musing way. —I don't know, but you people seemed pretty well played out. There's no money for your period. Oh a little trickles in for studies on Crosby or perhaps Carl Van Vechten. You know if you people had written more about each other, critical studies, monographs, we might be able to interest more people in you. But with just those few books and most of them, well. . . .

He looked at them and then he looked up at the corrugated ceiling of his office. In the waves of steel were dark clots of spider webs. —Maybe you should try some of the bookstores around here. Sometimes Authors are in them, signing their books.

He stood up and regarded them with a cheerful expression. —We do have a course in the critics, he said brightly. —I believe you people knew some of them: Winston Weethers, Jasper Gush, Eddy Ervine. You were pals with some of them, weren't you? He walked over and cleaned off a window in front of the silent quartet.

—Sometimes I think you people were anti-social that way, he said, more to himself than to them, —but it's too late now to do anything about it. Besides, what with the cutbacks. . . .

*—Whose idea was that, anyway?*

—Calm down, Scott, it was a stab in the dark.

—Hemingway!

—You mean a stab in the *pit,* don't you Ernest?

Ernest was trying not to look at Gertrude. —I mean, we had to try it out at least once.

—You know what I told you about those, Hemingway. No cliches.

Ernest regarded Gertrude with a pained expression.

—Look, I was just talking.

—Talking may not be literature, Hemingway, but you can always pretend, and practice.

—Yes, can't you, F. Scott put in, poking Ernest and rolling up his eyes.

—What did you mean by *that?*

—Gertrude, Alice said, putting her arm around Gertrude, —now there's no need for you to get into a literary. . . .

—I want to know. What did you mean by *that?*

Gertrude shrugged off Alice's arm and faced Ernest and F. Scott defiantly. She was pissed.

F. Scott smiled at her. It was a gentle smile, the smile that a crocodile smiles before it goes underwater for the kill.

—I meant, Gertrude, that you *did* acquire quite a reputation for turning *your* remarks into literature. I mean, *really.* . . .

Gertrude's face went pale. Then she nodded once. She took Alice's arm and began marching off toward Sather Gate. —We will find our way home by ourselves, she said, without turning back.

Ernest and F. Scott watched them cross the plaza. Gertrude had a curious hip-rolling walk, and mentally F. Scott began playing with it . . . like a camel with two broken legs in splints . . . no, like a. . . .

—Jesus, how huffy can you get? You'd think she could still write. That's the way she acts . . . like she wasn't immortal and could still write, when she knows she can't anymore. . . . It'd violate her contract.

—We're in the same boat, Ernest. But you know how Gertrude is: write as I say, not as I do.

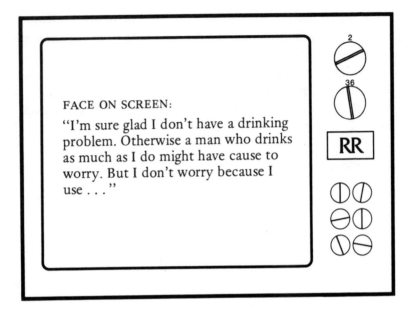

FACE ON SCREEN:

"I'm sure glad I don't have a drinking problem. Otherwise a man who drinks as much as I do might have cause to worry. But I don't worry because I use . . ."

VOICEOVER:

This is commonly known as SOLID GROUND. This man's argument is said to be standing on SOLID GROUND (and hence the name of the product). For those viewers who are hooking the cable up to their sinuses in order to receive ETERNAL / INTERNAL TELEVISION, please note the following carefully. When this man comes to your door, will you want to give him answers to his questions? Yes, you will. Because he's here to help you.

NOW FOR THE NEWS: *Some Say Yes*, starring Walt & Eric . . . "What we have been watching tonight is an ah uh *example* of brainwashing very rudimentary of course but still brainwash-

ing now in the following commentary there will be a single
train of brainwashing material running all the way through the
words you will hear try to find it in Reader A's running line
of commentary."

Reader A is a man about 26 who looks like he needs a new
sweater standing in a pile of leaves he smiles and nods once
as if you've just been talking perhaps you've even been old
friends and you're out for a walk with this man in a worn old
sweater friendly and frayed like your old sweater who is an
old friend and you find him talking to you as if you had been
talking recently maybe even already talking perhaps you've

—FLICK—

"Levitate the Lunch Gears, Doctor. Please refer to . . . *nurse!*
I want a nurse now, please give me back *my* nurse! I had a *fine*
nurse, a nurse who saw me naked in the morning and whose
heart *thrilled* as I whirled my cast above my head and bounced
up and down, up and down, on my bed—"

—FLICK—

Walt: "BACK OF THE CAMERA YOU WILL SEE

                              THE GIRAFFES
WHO HAVE BEEN WATCHING

                   THE SHOOTING.

                           THEY ARE
CURIOUS BEASTS AND

               THEY LIKE TO NUDGE THE CAMERAMEN

IN THE SHOULDER

    AS IF TO SAY

       "HEY,

         WHEN ARE WE GOING

TO GET ON TV?"

Eric: "YES, WALT,

      AND WHAT IS EVEN MORE AMAZING ABOUT

THIS IS THAT

    OUR CAMERA CREWS WERE

        *SO CAREFUL*

ABOUT THE LAND,

    THE PEOPLE,

       THE TOTAL ECOLOGY OF THE

PLACE, THAT THEY HAD

     *ANOTHER*

        GIRAFFE WHO WAS SKILLED

IN LANGUAGES,

    WHO COULD TRANSLATE

        AT A MOMENT'S

NOTICE

  *EXACTLY* WHAT THE GIRAFFES WERE SAYING."

Walt: "DID THEY EVER TALK, ERIC?"

Eric: (laughing heartily), "NO, WALT, THEY DIDN'T."

Walt: (facing camera), "AND NOW IN THE FREE BUSH SQUEAK OF BETTER DAYS AHEAD SAYS INVISIBLE IN THE SKY? SOME SAY YES. AND THAT'S THE WAY IT WAS, TODAY, MONDAY . . .

F. Scott and Ernest got up off the couch and walked across the student lounge.

—Isn't TV something? Ernest said.

—I can never remember what happens though, F. Scott said.

—It doesn't matter, Ernest said, —you're not supposed to.

—Where shall we look for Sherwood now? He wasn't in the news, F. Scott asked.

—Let's look over in the bookstores. Sherwood still reads books, and he likes to find used copies of his novels, Ernest said. —That's about the only place you can find his novels: in used bookstores.

—Look, F. Scott said, —I'll go over to the Pig Breeding Reactor and then maybe stop by the English Department.

—Where's the English Department?

—It's that alabaster diamond building over there. Standing up on one corner, like it's about to teeter off and crash down on the plaza. See it? Looks like a big white alabaster diamond balancing on one corner.

—Lot better-looking than the other one. That one looked like something left over from the First World War.

—I think that's how they regard American Literature too, like something left over.

Ernest Hemingway had his Temptation while he was thinking about that huge, beautiful English Department building
and why it was so white and perfect while the American
Literature building was so small and dingy.

He was standing by the water fountain in Sproul Plaza
pondering on it. The plaza was almost empty. A Saint Bernard stood in the water beside Ernest, peeing. The dog was
very happy to be standing in the water: his tongue was loll-
ing out and he was panting. It was a hot day in Berkeley.

Suddenly the Saint Bernard became a shelf of the most
beautiful edition of Shakespeare that Ernest had ever seen.
It made Ernest think he was in Heaven just to look at it.
And when he looked down, away from its beauty, he saw
that all he had to do was step into the pond and pick up
the Duo-Flex X-17 spear gun leaning against the edge of the
fountain and. . . .

As he imagined stepping into the fountain, he could see
even more beautiful editions of authors whose names were
completely unknown to him, editions and names of which
he had no knowledge and they seemed so strange and rare,
he found himself unable to move. . . .

Even a pair of hipboots awaited him. He had only to
step into the fountain and they would miraculously cover
his legs and feet. . . .

*Are these the writers of the future?* he thought. A
spark of jealousy flitted up through the flue of his emotions.

Then, as he wavered there, indecisive almost to the
point of pleasure—a rare emotion for him—the editions
changed into a huge slope of white snow. He saw that he
would only have to step out, and a pair of skis would be on

his feet and he would be flying, flying down into the icy face of the air, cleaving through it. . . .

But as he reached for the ski pole, it turned into a fly rod. He thought he would break it, his grip was so hard, so he let go the minute he touched it, knowing that he hadn't really grasped anything. . . .

And the fly rod fell, slowly melting and filling out into the clear skin of a beautiful girl lying on her side, smiling at a book in her hands. She slid down her sunglasses, looked up over them at Ernest, and smiled.

But he suddenly found himself seeing too far into her smile . . . almost behind it, an eery feeling . . . and he saw himself outside her, outside the icy air of skiing, outside those beautiful rare books. . . .

They all began to flip past him like scenes from the window of an express train and he found himself wandering away from the fountain, his eyes squinting, a tremor in his lips.

CHAPTER SEVEN:

WALL-TO-WALL
ON ALL FOUR SIDES

Meanwhile, in the back of a white Dodge van speeding into the farmlands surrounding the University, Gertrude and Alice were regarding their captors.

It had been a silly thing to do, hitch-hiking. But they had stuck their thumbs out, and the first van that had come by had stopped. Two nice-looking men with nylon stockings over their heads had helped them into the back and then they'd been told that they were going to Paris and they had only to relax and everything would be all right.

At first Gertrude and Alice didn't notice that the van was heading south rather than west. They were busy questioning the two young men about what group or fraternity they belonged to and why they had those nylon stockings over their heads.

The young men didn't say much in return, just sat there clutching their black rifles and nervously looking over the driver's shoulder every time the van slowed.

Alice nudged Gertrude as Gertrude was about to ask them if they liked the ferry ride over to Paris. —You know, I think we've just been kidnapped, Alice said.

—In that case, Alice, it's best that we become ghosts and evaporate, Gertrude replied.

One of the young men stuck his rifle into Alice's face and said, —You no evaporate. You stay here.

—Why? said Gertrude. She knew she would rather talk than evaporate any day.

The two Japanese men stepped into the chamber and turned the red dial on the wall all the way around.

—Ten minutes, one said.

—Ten minutes, the other replied.

They disappeared.

Inside the clear plastic cage, Sherwood Anderson watched the two men slowly frizz out into thin air. The place was dark. The one-way walls had been switched to clear once the tourists had left. Sherwood could see that he was inside a huge warehouse. He noticed the wrappers, and a newspaper on the floor. Popcorn and the green sports-section of the *San Francisco Chronicle.*

When he turned around, he found the Japanese men were behind him, over by a buckboard. Sherwood regarded them warily and then sat down on a rock.

—You upset. Upset people here. You no upset no more?

Sherwood looked them up and down. They were dressed in identical suits. Dark gray and shiny. Narrow red ties. The one man who spoke had flat cheekbones and almost no sheen to his skin while the other man had high cheekbones and glossy skin.

—This Iowa. Ohio. Whatever you want. Food. Brook. The high cheekbones man indicated the brook meandering by the buckboard. —Upset no more.

—I didn't say I wanted to *stay* here, Sherwood said. —You guys rigged that hotel room and somehow got me.

The man with the flat cheekbones nodded and bowed. —Sighs more eloquent than words. You sign. We give. Time comes, we go to. . . .

A sharp nudge by the other man shut him up.

—Where am I going?

—No worry. You okay. You master American prose. We give you paper, pens, typewriter. You need things to do, but if lonely, we fix it up.

Sherwood walked over by the pond. Through the clear water he could see a brick dam to one side. A fish nosed under some weeds. In the reflection of the pond, Sherwood saw his face. How old did he look? What did it matter if he were trapped in some plastic cage with Ohio?

He turned around and saw the two men slowly frizzing out into nothing but wispy air. He looked out at the chamber to one side of the warehouse just as the two men were appearing inside it. As they reached full form, one of them reached out and flicked a switch. The walls of Sherwood's cage went opaque.

A crowd of curious students were gathered around the cardboard box sitting in the middle of Sproul Plaza by the fountain. Some were slowly moving around the box and looking at the different motifs on the sides.

On the front of the box was a childish wallpaper, depicting cowboys and Indians romping around on a dimensionless flat brown backround. Loops of lariats separated each group.

On the sides were two other motifs: labels of various liquors, mixed with hotel luggage labels. The underside of the armholes were stained with sweat and the labels had taken on a dark, leathery, varnished look.

—Whoever's in there has really been around, one of the students said.

On the back of the cardboard box was a movie poster for a Marlene Dietrich movie. Written across the poster was the message: "Good hunting, The Kraut."

The students didn't look in the headhole because they could hear someone in there crying.

Inside Ernest was having a good cry. After his Temptation, he had pulled his head in like a turtle and had a good cry. He felt horrible, as if his life were closing in on him like four walls. *Even when I'm immortal,* Ernest thought unhappily to himself, *I still get that old feeling. Why top myself when I only end up inside my walls again. So what if they're infinite!*

So Ernest was crying, and feeling better.

However, not all of the students were inspecting Ernest's package. Some of them, primarily the veterinarian students, were working over the Saint Bernard, giving it artifi-

cial respiration. It had been found in the fountain, keeled
over, drowning.

One of the veterinarian students was commenting on
the curious dehydration of the dog, as if its life substance
had been sucked out of it.

—How could it be almost drowned and dehydrated at
the same time? one of them mused out loud.

—Maybe went for a drink, fell in water tiredly, an orien-
tal gentleman said, observing the resuscitation efforts of the
students.

Inside the alabaster diamond, F. Scott Fitzgerald was marveling at the swell Eighteenth Century English Novel room. Embedded in the four walls were four Professors, one per wall.

Actually one was missing from his wall, and this gave F. Scott a chance to inspect the curious texture of the walls which form-fit each professor.

Through the thin rubber membrane on the wall's surface, he could see back into the office of the professor. He was at his desk, eating an apple. DR. F. CUDWORTH AUDEN was inscribed on the brass name-plate underneath the hole.

*Actually,* F. Scott decided, *that wall's texture reminds me of a condom.*

Without the professor standing in the hole filling out the molded form of the wall-covering, the material looked exactly like a condom.

*A new condom,* F. Scott thought a little hurriedly.

To divert himself from *that* line of thought, F. Scott imagined the man eating an apple while inside the rubber wall, but somehow that didn't help much either, as the idea of a man eating an apple inside a condom was too absurdly symbolic of the Fall from the Garden of Eden. . . .

One of the other walls was delivering a lecture on Daniel Defoe. Or at least F. Scott thought it might be a lecture on him. He couldn't be sure because the lecture was almost entirely about change: how they used to make change; where they carried change; the function of change; ribald change jokes; what kinds of change you could get; who was more likely to have lots of change; change and manners; where change was changed into currency; change as an indicator of social status; and the rapid change of change. And somewhere in there Daniel Defoe's name was mentioned.

F. Scott watched as the man's mouth moved. The wall's membrane was completely molded around his features, and every gesture was easily accommodated by the membrane. There were a few students sitting on the rug below the Professor, taking notes.

F. Scott inspected the other two professors embedded in their walls. Both were staring out stoically as the lecture on change continued. One looked a little miffed.

—Do you like being encased in a wall? F. Scott said to the miffed Professor, —You know there's a great Edgar Allen Poe story about that.

The man didn't deign to notice him. F. Scott looked down at his name-plate, but the man's feet were so large that they stuck out far enough from the wall to obscure the entire name.

F. Scott didn't want to get down on his hands and knees to look at it, so he moved over to the other professor-wall. This one had a slick patina of white hair over his balding bullet-head, a big round pair of eyeglasses; he was wearing a top coat *and* a waistcoat. He was fingering an enormous watch in his waistcoat pocket, glancing down at it from time to time as his little pink nose twitched and twitched.

—Why doesn't the American Literature department have something like this? asked F. Scott. —I mean, this is some alabaster diamond.

—If he keeps this up, I'm . . . I'm going to be *late!* the little fellow said, nervously tugging his watch out from his vest pocket and fretting over it. —I just know it. I'm late.

I'm supposed to be in the 19th Century! What *am* I doing here? I'm late already.

F. Scott turned away from him and spied a slew of Graduate Program brochures on the table in the middle of the room. He picked up one and in reading it learned that a Japanese camera firm had funded the building of the alabaster diamond. It said in the pamphlet that this was done to further the study of English literature: something F. Scott hadn't thought was of much interest to the Japanese.

Inside the stone farmhouse about three miles south of the campus, the band of terrorists was busy putting blankets over the windows and sandbagging the side doors. At each window a terrorist was placing various weapons and ammunition. In the center of the living room the lead terrorist was giving orders. He was dressed exactly like the others: black pants, black bowling shirt with the identifying script ripped off and blacked-over with shoe polish, and a nylon stocking over the head with nose- and mouth-holes cut out.

Gertrude and Alice were watching with interest from the bedroom. Then their guard shut the door and began talking to them in English.

—Lucky you guys no hurt, Ha! We lucky to get you. Drive around three, maybe four days, looking for famous people. Very lucky. Hiroshi and me know you. Ha! Famous authors hitcha. Hitchahika. You stay put. Good. Maybe you help write demands.

Gertrude looked impassive. Alice nudged her. —So they know you in Japan, she whispered. Gertrude's face flushed a little and then she smiled.

—Certainly, she said to the terrorist, —I would be happy to help you write your list of demands. Just tell me what they are, and I will help you write them down.

—We know later. Not sure yet what demands are. First we find famous people to kidnap. Then demands.

—Isn't that backward? Alice put in.

—You no say that.

—Oh. Alice looked over at Gertrude and shrugged. —I thought terrorists knew what they wanted before they kidnapped anybody.

—How you write?

Gertrude raised her head and regarded the small man dressed completely in black. —You mean, what is my method?

—Yes. How to write. Their guard set his rifle on the floor in front of him and sat down crosslegged. —I read, many times, you. No make sense.

—Ah, Gertrude said, —then you went to college.

—Can not say backrounds. Go ahead. How to write.

—Well first of all, Gertrude said, fixing her eyes on the blank wall above her captor's head, —I know what poetry and prose have been and I have been telling this thing telling what poetry and prose have been and when I told it I said it in this way. . . .

Gertrude cleared her throat, and half an hour later, as Gertrude was still talking, Alice nudged her and whispered in her ear.

—Keep talking, Lovely. It's hard to tell, but I think he's fallen asleep. With that black nylon stocking over his head it's hard to tell, but I think he's asleep. Then we can get his rifle.

—Does telling anything as it is being needed being telling now by any one does it mean cutting loose from anything, why should we want his rifle this is exciting, no because there is nothing to cut loose from. We have no need of rifles.

Gertrude paused and regarded her captor. His head was hanging down, nodding every now and then. She lifted her head and stared at the blank wall as if it were a blank page and she began speaking again.

—It is funny that Americans that an American who has always believed that they were the people knowing everything about repression are really the ones who have naturally been moving in the direction that there is nothing to cut loose from. It is funny that Americans that an American who has always believed that they were the people knowing everything about repression are really the ones who have naturally been moving in the direction that there is nothing to cut loose from.

In the shitkicker's favorite bar in Emeryville, Ernest and F. Scott were putting the finishing touches on an afternoon's drinking. Both of them were embarrassed. Ernest over being found by F. Scott hiding inside his package, and F. Scott over finding Ernest crying inside his cardboard package. Drinking helped them both get over that experience, and before they were over it, they were drunk.

So there they were, at the Vegas Room in Emeryville, on the waterfront across the San Francisco Bay from Paris, sitting with the busted gamblers and truck-drivers, drinking and listening to Jim Reeves's song, *Four Walls.*

They'd both reached a silent time in their drunk. F. Scott's face was completely white. He was about to try to hire a drunken iron-worker down the bar to drive them back to San Francisco, since he'd just fired his own chauffeur. Ernest's face was red. He was about to write a bad poem in free verse on a napkin.

—Well. . . . F. Scott said after momentarily rejecting the idea of hiring an iron worker to drive his Cord roadster, —I guess Sherwood's not here.

Ernest concentrated on the bar napkin in front of him. He took out a ballpoint pen from one of the flaps in his cardboard box which doubled as a pocket, and clicked the point into position.

—Have been here for a couple of hours now. I wonder where Sherwood's gone to? F. Scott wondered out loud.

—Ya want it on? The Bartender reached behind a cardboard Bromo-Seltzer display on the bar, and flicked on the television above the bar. —Get the news. That's all that's on, if that's what ya want, the Bartender said, mostly to himself.

About five minutes into the news, just when F. Scott had become convinced that his right foot was hidden somewhere under his bar stool (he didn't know how to get off the stool with only one foot and go look for it, let alone put it back on); and as Ernest was about halfway through with his poem and had turned over the bar napkin to finish it, much to the relief of F. Scott, who had been secretly reading the poem (and finding it too awful for words), the newscaster gave a little chuckle and came to the humorous segment of the news show.

—Things don't change much in the land of radical agripolitics over there at the University of Iowa in Berkeley. Today the police there received a communique from the group calling themselves "The Better Homes Akimbo" group, a self-styled anti-property terrorist cooperative. The communique read as follows:

*Attention Capitalist Home-Owners and World Suppressionists. We are holding two famous writers: Gertrude Stein and Alice B. Toklas. We are holding them well. Each of them is well. We are ready to defend our position that we hold as well.*

The newscaster smiled and then held up a piece of paper. —And what follows this is a list of demands in what might be described as a stream of broken English, leading the police to believe that the terrorists are not native Americans. While the police are trying to decipher the communique, they are also trying to solve another problem: both Gertrude Stein *and* Alice B. Toklas are *dead*. Is it a hoax? This is what police chief Charley Half-Gainer had to say about that to our Eyewitness newsteam:

A fat-faced man with a microphone in his hand and much perspiration on his face was blinking as bright lights swept across his face and then zeroed in on him. Microphones were waving around in front of him.

—We are informed
that while we believe the two named ah
writers are *believed*
to be *dead,*
we think that this group
the ah Better Homes Akimbo
ah group,
is *serious*
and they are holding two hostages,
dead *or* alive.
We will make all efforts
to secure the *release*
of these two hostages,
whether, as I have said,
they are American citizens,
*foreign* citizens,
or dead or whatever. . . .

—They didn't say anything about Sherwood, Ernest said sharply, pushing his bar napkin away from him. —I think we better get over to the police station and find out what is going on.

Ernest stood up and moved soddenly away from the bar. As F. Scott got up from his bar stool, his right leg crumpled under him. He fell heavily against Ernest, creasing his package, and then plopped onto the floor.

—Jesus Christ, Scott, get up.

—Lost my foot, Ernie. I keep losing my body. I'm fall-ing apart. . . . Let's hire that iron-worker to drive us back to San Francisco, Ernie.

—It's on the other end of your leg, you asshole.

—He is? F. Scott looked down at his leg but he didn't see the iron-worker there. —Is that why I can't walk? Can't use an iron-worker for a foot, can I? Scott giggled.

—No, your foot: your foot's on the end of your leg. Now get up before this group decides to make a move on you. They already think you're a nance, with your pretty linen suit. And forget about that iron-worker, he's not going to be hired by *you.*

At the police station the pair was directed to the out-skirts of South Berkeley, where the main cash-crop was hops. Ernest drove the Cord up a hop-lined drive to the big square white house with the swooping gray roof: a classic midwest-ern house. Ringed around it were police vehicles and police with shotguns, rifles, and automatic weapons.

Inside the farmhouse the tallest terrorist with the black nylon over his head was waving the newspaper at Gertrude and Alice and screaming.

—You see? TV too! *No understand,* Gertrude Stein! Radio! *No way Gertrude Stein,* no one understand!

—What's he saying? Alice asked Gertrude. They were sitting on the bed holding each other's hand. —I don't know, Gertrude said.

The terrorist shook the piece of newspaper in their faces and backed up. —No, no, no one knows!

—What don't they understand?

—Better Homes Akimbo Communique No. 1! the terrorist screamed. —No, no one understand! Why don't they understand?

—I don't know, Gertrude said, very composed, —but they will.

—They *will!* The terrorist began jumping around the room gnawing at the edges of the newspaper. —They will! they will! ahh-ahhhhh-ahhhhhh!

—Yes. Later, Gertrude said, nodding. —They will understand it much later but then they will understand it much better.

—No time for later! Surrounded by police! Police everywhere! We die. You die. Say what we say, but say it better. Yes?

Gertrude drew herself up and regarded him coldly.

—I've said what I said and I am not going to say it anymore.

Just then the first tear gas grenade exploded through the small wire opening in the foundation directly underneath the living room floor and the coughing fart of its detonation sent the leader rushing back from their room.

—Attack! Ready! and then he lapsed into rapid Japanese screaming.

The front window, which had been boarded up, dissolved under a stream of high-velocity machine gun bullets. The Better Homes Akimbo group-leader found his stomach shredded into strips of bloodied meat. His legs and hips dropped on the floor as his shoulders and head bounced against the wall and fell down like the top of a discarded mannequin.

—This man says he will negotiate for their release and pay any ransom, the police lieutenant was saying in a whisper to Ernest as they crouched behind the Cord.

—I don't remember any ransom being asked for, Ernest whispered back.

—It might be in there. So far we haven't been able to figure out what the fuck their message means.

—Then why is this guy here?

—He says he will ransom this Stein and her friend Toklas. That's all he says.

Ernest looked down the lane at the parked Cadillac and the crowd of police moving traffic along the road. A small man in a gray suit was looking down the lane at the white house. He had an attache case in his hands.

—Lawyer?

—Maybe.

—You have his name?

—Yeah. Think it's worth a try. Do Stein and Toklas know anyone who would automatically ransom them?

Ernest was about to answer when the first burst of gunfire came ringing through the trees and the cough of a shotgun was heard repeatedly.

The walls of Sherwood Anderson's cage went clear again and he found himself staring at the back of a man's head and a ring of television cameras. A man in a white canvas chair behind the cameras and lights stood up and nodded.

—Hello, welcome to Writerland. Writerland is proud to present its first live author: Sherwood Anderson. Sherwood Anderson is a well-loved American author who wrote the classic WINESBURG OHIO. Here you see him in his native Midwestern habitat. Dabbling in a pond, musing on a buckboard, Sherwood Anderson lived the life of a writer in his native country, returning often to the Midwest for fresh inspiration.

—Okay. Cut. Look more outward, lift your head, that's right, up, up, no, down, chin down a little. Right. Now outward.

—Hello, welcome to Writerland. Writerland is proud to present its first live author: Sherwood Anderson. Sherwood Anderson is a well-loved American author who wrote the classic WINESBURG OHIO. Here you see him in his native Midwestern habitat. Dabbling in a pond, musing on a buckboard, Sherwood Anderson lived the life of a writer in his native country, returning often to the Midwest for fresh inspiration.

Sherwood stared down at the back of the man's head. The director stood up and waved the man over a bit and readjusted the lights. Then the man in front of Sherwood's cage read the speech again, but this time in Japanese. Then a young girl came up and stood where the man had been standing and read the speech again, in French and German.

When the man walked away, Sherwood saw his face. It

was a normal face. Sherwood sat on the buckboard and watched as the girl finished her speeches. She had a normal face too. When she finished her speeches, she left. A small man with a normal face came up and spoke in Chinese.

A pair of workmen followed him and placed a gleaming glass counter in front of the cage. Sherwood walked over and stared down at it. In the case were all the notebooks and manuscripts and books that he had used from time to time.

Then two Japanese men came in carrying a seven-foot-high wax statue of Abraham Lincoln and placed it alongside the counter. The statue was partially electric too: one arm could raise in a semi-fascist salute, and the mouth moved up and down as the following words were broadcast:

HOWDY ILLINOIS

First in English. Then in Japanese. French and German and Chinese. Illinois stayed the same throughout. Howdy kept changing.

F. Scott and Ernest both retreated to the road as the firing
became intense. The police were crawling on the ground a-
round the house, sneaking from cover to cover. A grenade
went off under a huge elm tree to one side of the house and
bits of black rubbish flew up against the green leaves.

—We'd better get behind the squad car, Ernest said as
stray bullets stitched a hem of dust on the road. —We're way
too close for this kind of action.

—Traffic dandy, the Japanese gentleman in the dark pin-
striped suit said to them as they ducked behind the car.

—What?

—I said traffic's dandy for shooting. Bing! Bing! No
cars, but many, many bullets. He grinned.

—Ah, yeah, Ernest said, turning back to F. Scott, —Say
does it ever bother you that people are sometimes identical
to their stereotypes?

—You mean like Lincoln on the five-dollar bill?

—Right. I'd sure hate to have to write about these guys
like this guy now. The ethnic types would jump all over my
ass.

The police lieutenant came scuttling down the road and
hunkered down beside Ernest for a moment. —That's the
guy, he said, nodding toward the Japanese gentleman. He
rolled over into the ditch behind the car and took a position
behind a rock.

From the farmhouse came the sounds of small arms
fire. A stream of smoke was coming up from the back.

—The chief here tells me you were the one to put up
the ransom money, if any: How come?

—Not at liberty to tell that.

—Your clients?

—Yes, we like to keep that confidential.

—What's their interest in Gertie?

—American Literature. My clients are interested in American Literature. They desire to remain anonymous.

—Talks pretty good now, doesn't he? Ernest said, turning to F. Scott and then, as he turned back to the lawyer, carefully took his attache case out of his hands. —Thank you.

The Japanese lawyer was outraged. His nostrils flared and his eyes grew round as Ernest carefully opened up the case and took out the envelope marked *Stein & Toklas.* —You better hand that back quick. He scuttled backwards and tensed up.

—Real good English, Scott, Ernest said, slitting the envelope open with a thumbnail.

—AHHHHHHHHHHHHHHHHH YA! the lawyer screamed, leaping at Ernest, hands spread out in twin karate chops.

But just as he was flying through the air above the car to garrot Ernest, the entire white farmhouse exploded and the shrapnel and blast sent him careening back into the drainage ditch in back of the police car.

—Jesus Christ, Ernest said, hugging the side of the rocking police car. —What happened?

Where the farmhouse had been, only a squat round gray cloud of dust now mushroomed out under the splintered elm trees. Bits of branches still swung back and forth in the smoke. Sections of the four walls were wrapped around the tree trunks.

Police cars were overturned all around the farmhouse. Men were crawling and waving and shouting. The police holding back traffic on the road were all running toward the cloud of smoke and the wasted farmhouse. The lieutenant jumped up from behind the car and joined the frantic race up the lane toward the disaster.

F. Scott and Ernest watched from behind the patrol car. Ernest brought the check out of the envelope and stared at it.

—What was the name of that camera company, the one that built the alabaster diamond for the University?

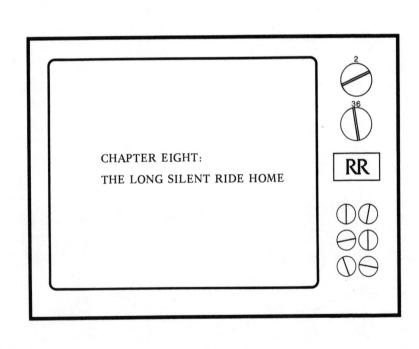

CHAPTER EIGHT:

THE LONG SILENT RIDE HOME

It was a long and silent ride back home for Ernest and F. Scott. Each was deep in thought.

On the ferry, both Ernest and F. Scott were deep in thought. It was a long silent ride home.

Home on the ferry. A long silent ride.

On the ferry, both Ernest and F. Scott found it a long silent ride.

Ferrying back home, F. Scott and Ernest rode, each deep in thought.

Deep in thought on the ferry ride home: F. Scott and Ernest.

Home on the ferry with long silent deep thoughts: F. Scott Fitzgerald and Ernest Hemingway each riding home.

F. Scott. Ernest. Deep thoughts riding home on the long silent ferry.

O to be riding home on the ferry with Ernest and F. Scott, each riding deep in long silent thoughts.

While they were riding on the ferry, Ernest and F. Scott had
an imaginary conversation. It went something like this:
 —Well, let's look at it from our point-of-view.
 —Right.
 —Sherwood disappears from his hotel room in Paris,
leaving only two blue handmade socks. A Madame Christine
is involved but can't be found. Both you and Gertrude seem
to have petite visions around the same time. Then Gertrude
and Alice are captured by Better Homes Akimbo. A guy
from Yoshimura Camera Company comes up with the ransom money for them, even though the terrorists didn't de-
mand any money, at least from what I read of the
communique.
 —You say you saw it?
 —Yeah, the lieutenant there showed me a copy of it.
It was pure Gertie. Abstract as hell and full of pronouns.
Didn't say anything about money.
 —Well, here's a question: why would Gertrude write the
communique for her captors?
 —You got me. But it was Gertie's prose all right. I
know it when I can't read it.
 —So where's that leave us?
 —Nowhere. And on top of that, now *I'm* having visions.
 —Well, Ernest, as a plot it stinks. So far Sherwood's un-
connected with Gertie's kidnapping. There's no reason we
can see why she should have written the communique. Our
only leads are that check and Madame Christine.
 —Yeah, this check. Maybe we oughta take this check
back to them and say we found it in the fields out there.
 —Say we found it alongside a tattered karate chop.

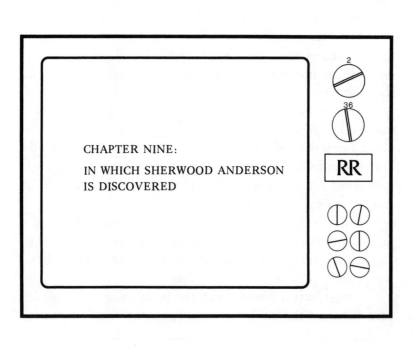

CHAPTER NINE:

IN WHICH SHERWOOD ANDERSON
IS DISCOVERED

The first thing Ernest and F. Scott did was to set up their own detective agency. Smitty flew down to L.A. to check out the Yoshimura Camera Company. He said he had a friend who had access to various computer listings. Then F. Scott went out to get some business cards and stationery printed up while Ernest and F. Scott's new chauffeur, Denis Kelly, began canvassing North Beach for an office.

The only place they could find was an apartment, at 314 Union St. All the office space around was taken, so they decided to work out of the apartment.

It had just been vacated, but not entirely. A tall blond man with a full beard and a droopy mustache was moving out his last belongings when Ernest and Denis arrived with their new office furniture.

They supervised the men from the furniture store as they moved in the equipment. The tall blond man stood to one side holding a garishly-painted papier-mache bird and a fly-fishing rod as a filing cabinet was wheeled by him.

The phone rang. —That must be yours, the tall blond man said, —mine was disconnected yesterday. He started down the stairs with the papier-mache bird. —That step ladder's going too, he said, nodding toward a short step-ladder with a red velvet fringe on top. There was a snow shovel leaning against it.

Ernest answered the phone. —Yes, oh yeah, all moved in, do you have the cards? Great. Come on over, right. 314 Union. No, Smitty hasn't called yet. Right. It's right below my place, Coit Tower. Uh-huh. Bye.

Ernest busied himself with the positioning of the desks, then followed the tall blond man down the stairs, as he carried the step ladder and the snow shovel outside and put them into a chalky green 1953 Chevy pickup.

As the man put the gear in back, Ernest noticed that the packing crates in back were all marked RB/5-7-1-806 Hiroo, shibuya-ku, Tokyo 150 Japan.

—You going to Japan? Ernest asked the driver, a mustached fellow in a derby hat who vaguely reminded him of Teddy Roosevelt.

—I'm not, the driver said. —He is, nodding toward the tall blonde man beside him.

Just as they pulled out down Union St., Ernest saw F. Scott getting out of a cab down by the grocery store at Kearny and Union. He waited for him to come up the hill.

—Here they are, F. Scott said, handing Ernest a box of business cards. He was slightly out of breath from the climb.

Ernest opened them up as they walked to the office. They were printed in red and black ink. In large bold red letters on the top of the card were the words:

# RHINO RITZ

### TROUBLESHOOTERS

E. RHINO                                    F.S. RITZ

526-1629

—Nice work, Scott.

—You heard from Smitty yet?

—No, but I'm expecting a call any minute.

The two busied themselves with arranging their respective offices. The call came at two that afternoon.

Ernest put down the phone. —He's got the goods. I think a few things are beginning to fall into place now. Ernest nodded at F. Scott. —I think we're going to make short work of this caper.

—Anything else?

Ernest looked out the window at the Eiffel Tower. —He said the bulls were running in the canals at Venice, but the boatmen were excellent at avoiding them. If we can wrap this up in a few days, we might head down there for the fiesta.

Later that night, high atop Coit Tower in Ernest and Ku-na-so-way's teepee, F. Scott and Ernest and Smitty discussed the facts. Smitty had a long computer readout of all the holdings of the Yoshimura Camera Company. He also had several recent articles in trade papers and scientific magazines about the current projects that the company was embarked on. They sat crosslegged on the floor as the pipe went a-round. In the middle of them was the welter of paper from Smitty's gleanings. Just to the right of Ernest and slightly behind him Ku-na-so-way sat with a bag of tobacco.

—Did you see this one, Smitty?

—No, which one is that?

—The one on screenless movies. Movies that they've de-veloped that don't need a screen to be shown. Look, it's in the experimental stage but they can show movies on the windows of taxis, on a fish, anything. Actually what they seem to be doing is showing the movie on an object or on a person's aura. They call it the P.O.V. machine.

F. Scott waited until Smitty finished glancing over the article and then he traded him the pipe for it. He looked at the first page hard for about 30 seconds and then he flipped the page and 30 seconds, 30 seconds, and the article was done.

—Reading that awfully fast, aren't you?

—I took a speed-reading & -writing course when I was in Hollywood.

—What do you think?

F. Scott shrugged. —It says that it's not in use yet. Still in the experimental stage. Says it sometimes damages the ob-jects that are used as screens, especially if used too long.

—I think it's been in use, Scott. Remember that absinthe?

F. Scott looked stunned for a moment and then he pulled his astonishment down out of his face as if his mind were blinking. —Of course, he said.

—Of course, he said.

—And my St. Bernard.

—Your St. Bernard?

Ernest explained the scene at Sproul Plaza to Smitty, omitting a few details toward the end.

—Big aura there. But the dog was wiped-out afterwards—or that's what I was told.

—You were told? Smitty looked confused.

—Well, yes, told. I was a little shook-up with the whole thing so I was looking the other way. . . . Ernest glanced over at F. Scott. —And Gertrude's *Collected Works,* don't forget them. Probably they tried to show them through the door; doesn't it say there they can do that too? And it wasn't strong enough, so she thought she was just imagining it, naturally. Gertrude never was too strong on visual imagining so she dismissed it as a minor hallucination, just as you dismissed your absinthe streetlight as a minor vision.

—But why would anybody, especially a Japanese camera company (if that's who is doing it), want to show us those things?

—They're all temptations, you dummy: I thought that was your field.

F. Scott was about to say something when Smitty broke in. —Why should anybody want to tempt you? Especially if it's just a movie. You can't *have* the things, obviously.

—Yeah, but there's a kind of hypnosis involved, right?
F. Scott said, picking up the article again. —Says here anyway that some subjects are, well, seduced I guess, into believing it. Sorta like the movies. But it seduces your Point
of View, your P.O.V.

—But Smitty's got a point. That's what we've got to
find out: *why.*

—And if it *is* this company, F. Scott said.

Ernest handed the pipe back to Ku-na-so-way and she
began filling it. There was a silence as Smitty and F. Scott
watched Ku-na-so-way carefully wipe the shreds of tobacco
off the bowl's edge then hand it back to Ernest. Ernest patiently held it as she took a Zippo from her leather jerkin
and lit it for him.

—I think it's got to do with American Literature. American Writers. Whoever got Sherwood wanted to get us too.

—But for what? We can't write anymore. It's in the
contract.

Ernest regarded F. Scott skeptically. —Well . . . he said,
now Sherwood knew that, and I found this item in his
dresser. . . .

—Oh come on, Ernest. You know the deal. We get to
be immortal and all that but no more books. Besides, you
know what happens if we do.

Ernest drew himself up inside his package and began to
stare at the complete Charles Dickens that was tanned and
mounted on the wall behind F. Scott's head. It was clear
that he didn't want to talk about it.

—What we've got to do, he began saying precisely, each
syllable pronounced crisply, —is tail the guy who runs the

aura movie projector or P.O.V. Machine or whatever it's called, here in San Francisco.

F. Scott leaned back and regarded Ernest with an amused expression. —Uh huh, maybe you ought to do that, Rhino. He'll never notice a man in a cardboard box following him around.

—Look Scott, I know you're smarter than I am. . . .

—Now wait a minute, back off a little. You guys let me do the tailing. I already know the guy's name, it's right here. Smitty scanned a readout and pointed to a gray line on it. —M. Michael Soul.

—So what are *we* going to do, Rhino?

—Fuck you, Scott.

—Come on, Smitty said.

—The one piece that doesn't fit is the abduction. Why were Gertrude and Alice spirited off? Why did they help write the communique? And why did the camera company want to ransom them, especially if they're behind this temptation business?

—Well, maybe those guys were terrorists, I mean, *really* terrorists.

—Look, Smitty said, —why don't you quit arguing and just go find out from them?

In the morning Ernest met Smitty and F. Scott at the Cafe
Trieste for coffee. During the night F. Scott had picked up
a small dark woman with an incredibly delicate face. She
was silent and seemed almost completely pleased, unlike the
new chauffeur, Denis Kelly. He was obviously just coming
off a night's drinking with F. Scott, and was nervously waiting for the first creak of the hangover in his body.

—Top of the morning to you, he said to Ernest, pulling
on his scraggly brown beard and winking.

After coffee, the woman said goodbye to F. Scott and
slipped off toward Columbus Avenue as they all traipsed up
the hill to the office. There they split up the details.

Smitty went off to tail Michael Soul, the camera company illusions man. F. Scott and his chauffeur were to scout
out various buildings that Yoshimura owned in San Francisco and Paris.

Ernest walked down to his bank, took out several hun-
dred dollars in small bills, and flagged down a taxi just as
soon as he stepped out into the crisp San Francisco morning
air.

His first stop was the Foster's across from the A.C. Transit bus terminal. No one was in the cafeteria, so he legged it
across the street and checked out the sundries counter in
Terminal Drugs. No luck.

The next stop was a garage out in the Mission district.
Supposedly this was another spirit-drop, albeit for low-riding
spirits. There a man with a bald head and badly gimped leg
was working under the rear-end of a Studebaker as two Hells
Angels looked on.

—No, ain't seen no one. Been under this Studie all morning long.

The Hells Angels didn't say anything. They didn't even look like they were wasting time: they were abusing it. The gimp rolled back under the Studebaker.

Nairobi Wigs proved equally devoid of interest. Deciding to move another notch up the Spirit Drop Ladder, Ernest entered the Museum of Modern Art on MacAllister. He cruised the guards, but the only person of interest was an elevator man reading a newspaper with a big tennis shoe imprint in the middle of a lingerie ad.

Ernest crossed town and drove up Clement to the Russian Bakery. He had a piroshki and a cup of coffee and some bourme. All the waitresses were fat and white and dumpy and they all looked like someone's aunt. One had a small red button on her lapel which said, in Russian: "Don't ask me. I just work here."

As Ernest was leaving the bakery, he noticed the bookstore up the street. The Green Apple. As far as he knew it wasn't a spirit drop, but he eased up the street and checked out the 25¢ stalls. The first one had only nurse novels and political biographies and sexual advice for Baptist teenagers, which were putting in time there until the moment when Jean Paul Sartre died: then they would be shipped immediately to him for use in his post-mortality library.

The second stall was full of his own books, only each book cover was pitted with small indentations. Ernest inspected them closely and dug a BB out of a copy of *For Whom The Bell Tolls*.

—Whatta ya think of that, huh? How does it feel, Mr. Safari?

Ernest looked up to see the proprietor of the bookstore, John Vaglia, standing there in the doorway with a Daisy BB gun in his hand. With his bloodshot eyes and big beagle nose, he looked like an escaped hangover.

—Ya ever come in this goddamn bookstore again, you big freak, I'll fill your cardboard hide full of BB's. See that! That's the latest one and the last one. There'll never be another one of your books in my store again! He handed Ernest a copy of *The Torrents of Spring*. It was so pitted with BB holes it would have made a perfect model for an acne ad about adolescent books.

—Well, it's just a sport, Ernest began.

—Sport, my ass! Coming into my bookstore and shooting a big spear through my Stendhal. . . . Mr. Vaglia retreated into the store, muttering and wiping his nose.

Ernest turned back to the nearest bus stop and rode up to the Palace of the Legion of Honor. The place was almost empty. He spent about an hour there, checking out all the cooks in the cafeteria and the guards and the attendants. No luck.

As he was waiting for a cab, he stared at the back of Rodin's *Thinker*. The *Thinker*'s feet seemed too big and his back too short, but Ernest wasn't sure that this wasn't just the early morning light or his point-of-view. It was strange living in California.

Ernest wondered if people lost their perspective in California from time to time, everything being so opaque, just to have something to do.

—Fort Point, he said to the cabbie.

At the bottom of the road leading down to the fort, Ernest had the cab stop and he paid the driver. He told him to stick around if he wanted, it would only take a minute, and the cabbie said sure.

Fort Point was a strange brick fort overlooking the mouth of the San Francisco Bay. Above it the weird orange girders of the Golden Gate Bridge made the fort seem like a child's toy, slightly out-of-scale and whimsical. It had been built in the 1860s to fight off the imminent Confederate naval invasions, and like all creatures of California fantasy, it never lost its air of permanent unreality.

Inside the fort was even weirder than outside because the walls crimped together at odd angles and the battlements were empty and frail and ghostly. Standing in the middle of the grounds was like being in the head of a brick kaleidoscope: it felt like all the angled brick walls were about to jumble in on you.

Ernest followed the signs into the kitchen/office area and watched as Alice B. Toklas finished her lecture to a troop of Boy Scouts. The lecture was entitled "Cooking for the Army during the Civil War."

—How many other spirit drops did you try before you came here?

—A few. The wig shop on Haight, Terminal Drugs, the Foster's there, and that transmission repair shop in the Mission, just on the off chance that you'd show up there.

—Not me, certainly, Alice said, looking a little offended.

—No, I was thinking that Gertrude might end up there, what with her interest in cars. But then I began the rounds of the public museums and monuments.

—It's strange how most San Francisco public places are staffed by spirits in transit. Whole staffs of ghosts posing as guards, mostly artistic ghosts. I don't know any other city in the world. Why even Paris gives their guard jobs to veterans, but San Francisco . . . ghosts.

—Yeah, I saw what looked like Hart Crane selling postcards of the Golden Gate Bridge at the Legion. So where's Gertrude?

—She's out taking the children on a tour of the cannon and such. I think there'll be one more group coming in today and then we can go back to Paris.

—Well, this is what we've found out. It looks like a Japanese camera company might be behind this. At least connected. F. Scott and I have set up a dummy detective agency and are investigating.

Ernest handed Alice one of his cards.

—Oh how exciting. You know Gertrude just loves mysteries.

—You didn't hear anything from your captors about a Yoshimura Camera Company, did you?

—No, Alice said, We didn't. This is the way it
happened. . . .

Ernest listened to Alice's account. —Then you could
barely understand them?

—Yes, we actually had to write their communique for
them. Alice looked around the fort's kitchen and sighed.
—And Gertrude couldn't resist, so now we have to work out
our penalty time here.

Ernest shrugged. —Well, he said a little guiltily, thinking
of all the manuscripts he had hidden in his teepee, —a deal
is a deal. She pulled down time taking Boy Scouts around
just for publishing a little communique. Well. . . .

Alice looked resigned. —She still writes, of course, but
only on that paper they give you. It dissolves in the morning. We could have gotten some that I could have typed up,
just like old times, but I'm tired of typing Gertrude's
manuscripts. I didn't become Immortal just so I could con-
tinue typing manuscripts.

—Did you get blown up?

—No, we evaporated. Just as soon as we heard the
bullets.

—Do you think it was just *chance?*

Alice looked bewildered. —I don't know, Hemingway.
They said they had been driving around for days, looking
for famous people to kidnap, but we didn't know whether
to believe them.

Just then Gertrude Stein came in wearing a WWI army
cavalry uniform with jodhpurs and a peaked pinched-top
hat. In her hand were some tourist brochures. With her beau-

tiful severe face she looked like the Madonna of the Cavalry Recruiting Corps.

—Oh hello Hemingway. What's the news of the lost Sherwood? Have you found him yet?

Hemingway filled her in on the events she'd missed.

—I just think it was chance, she replied. —I don't see what or how our kidnapping was anything else. Isn't that funny, though? Here we are on a big case, a missing person's case, and something happens just by chance. Isn't that odd?

—Yeah, but we've learned a lot of things from it. Like the camera company. How long did you draw this time?

Gertrude looked irritated. —Oh, I don't know. I mean if it's okay to write grocery lists and to pass notes, why doesn't a little communique count as a note?

—Gertrude, Hemingway said soberly, —that little note was four typed pages.

—I had to type them, Alice said. —I was the only one who could read her writing.

—How did they like it? Was it well-received? Gertrude asked.

—Look Gertrude, let's not go into the literary reception of your communique. We were thinking that if your kidnapping were strictly a chance operation, then all the evidence points to the Yoshimura Company being in on Sherwood's nabbing.

—That's if he was nabbed, Hemingway. It could be chance, just like with us. Gertrude paused. —Tell me about those aura movies again. . . . And where *is* the P.O.V. machine?

Ernest shrugged. —I don't know. But I think that we're

being tempted so we will *do* something, *what* I don't know. I think it's . . . conditioning of some sort. Conditioning us to . . .

—To accept what? The conditions of the temptations?

—Why don't you go ask them? Alice put in, folding a kitchen towel.

—Maybe I'll go do that, Ernest said. —Try the direct approach. Just then the clamor of a bunch of young Boy Scouts came spilling through the open kitchen door. —Well, I leave you to your touring. When you're sprung from your punishment, let me know.

—Penance, Alice corrected him.

Hemingway left without answering. The Boy Scouts were milling on the parade grounds like a brigade of crazed dwarf Union soldiers.

Ernest refused to feel sorry for Gertrude. Free will is what feels good, he thought, and predestination takes care of the rest. The taxi was waiting. The taxi driver was reading P.G. Wodehouse.

—You know . . . you know I always thought being immortal was gonna be easy. But it's not. It's har'. F. Scott leaned against Denis and complained. —Not easy at all. Poor Gertrude. Poor Alice. Stuck in a museum.

—Are all those women of yours part of that too? Denis asked, propping up Scott with one arm. —I've never seen anything like it. You oughta get a stick to beat them off with.

—Yeaaaah, but I gotta take 'em to the Jack Tar Hotel. It's not exactly my style, but it's in my contract, you know.

They were standing outside the Japantown Wax Museum. In the display window was a wax replica of Elvis Presley. He had on an outfit actually worn during a performance in Las Vegas. Elvis was smiling, but the face in the wax looked puffy, and his smile made him look like an invisible dentist had a tool under his upper lip and was resting his index finger on the lower lip.

—Very har', F. Scott was saying to Denis who was holding him up and trying to nod agreement at the same time. —You know, I always thought being immortal was easy. I really did. But it's not. You know that?

—Well, right now it looks as hard as being alive, said Denis, trying to fish a cigarette out of his pocket and keep F. Scott on his feet.

—Very har'. Being immortal is very hard. Hard. You have to watch your P's and Q's, F. Scott said, wagging a finger in Denis' face.

Denis was trying to light a cigarette. For a moment F. Scott's finger and the lighter did a *pas de deux* as Denis tried to avoid searing Scott's pinkie.

—Uhhhmmmmmmm, Denis said, —why don't you lean against the wall over there by that poster while I buy us some tickets.

—Gotta mind your P's and Q's or else you gotta go into *the museum.*

—That's what we're trying to do now, so why don't you just lean over there on that poster and I'll buy us some tickets. Okay? That's it, just lean against that poster and I'll buy us some tickets.

F. Scott leaned against a poster for the Wax Museum. It showed King Kong and Willie Mays. King Kong had one hand raised in a salute to the little American flag flying in the corner of the poster. Willie Mays stood beside King Kong, holding a bat, and smiling. Underneath it said:

STARS OF AMERICAN ENTERTAINMENT WEEK FESTIVAL

Denis approached the ticket vendor's window. He brought out a wad of money and handed the man in the booth a five. The man had been watching them closely. He smiled. —Sorry, he said, —museum all closed for today. No come in. Come back tomorrow, okay? He pushed the five back at Denis.

Denis pushed the five back at him. —Someone just went in there.

The man smiled. He had a normal haircut for a Japanese. He was wearing a light blue shirt. —That last one, he said, easing the five back out the window to Denis.

Denis pushed the five back towards him. —Two tickets please.

—Sorry show closed now. Easy come back tomorrow.
OPen all the time tomorrow.

He pushed the money back at Denis and then added a
card to the money. Denis picked up the card and read it.

REAL ESTATE INVESTMENT
COMPUTERIZED LISTINGS & ANALYSIS


HU CHING


*Doctor of Science—Nuclear Engineering*
*Broker—Real Estate*
*Ticket-Taker*

—Thanks, Denis said, realizing the man was Chinese,
—but my man I don't want to buy any used nuclear plants
today. I'd like two tickets, he pushed the money in, —and
I'd like them right now.

Mr. Ching was still smiling. He was smiling so hard his
whole face looked like it was about to lift off and float a-
round the booth like a teeth-filled balloon.

—No got tickets. Run all out. No more tickets. What
can do? Closed. A shrug. —No tickets.

F. Scott squinted at Denis and then lurched over.

—What would you do if you slipped up, I mean,
slipped up the tiniest bit, just a bit of dialogue, and put it
out, say in the Reader's Digest, or something. A joke or

something. What's that? Nothing. But in you go. Blap! into the museums watching the tourists come and go in front of a silkscreen Chairman Mao. Do you know what that *does* to artists? he asked drunkenly.

Denis took F. Scott by the hair and pushed his head down on the counter. —This man will puke all over you and your counter if I don't have those two tickets immediately.

Mr. Ching regarded the face of F. Scott Fitzgerald pressed against his polished aluminum ticket dispenser and then he stopped smiling. He reached out and took the five and touched a button to the right of F. Scott's nose. Two tickets *hu-erred* out beside his head.

—Irish Terrorist Tactics, Denis remarked jovially to F. Scott as he helped him into the wax museum. —Fear of the Gut Splash. A Gaelic mystery. Yes, the fabled Puke Cannon defended the olde sod from many an invader. Prepare the Puke Cannon! To the breach! Drench the swine with filth! Hooray!

F. Scott began a hysterical giggle but the two guards who followed them around as they reeled from wax exhibit to wax exhibit were considerably less amused. They bungled around the place for a half an hour or so until F. Scott, who had been fascinated by the exhibits from the 1930s, suddenly straightened up. His most dignified English air slid into place in front of his drunkeness as if the alcohol had been rinsed from his system.

—I *say*. Denis, . . . but look here.

—Where?

—There, between those two Sioux Indians.

Denis and F. Scott both moved up a little closer to the

glass window and stared at the exhibit. In the canvas back-
drop of the scene (which depicted John Dillinger holding up
two Indians) there was a 4-inch tear. Through it could be
seen a solitary light shining down on a black cube about fif-
ty feet behind the canvas.

Written in script on top of the black cube were the
words SHERWOOD ANDERSON, 1876-1941. There was a large
dark figure next to the cube, wearing a stovepipe hat.

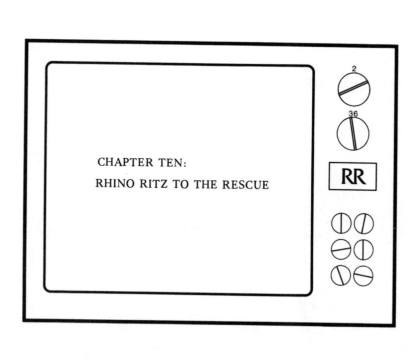

CHAPTER TEN:

RHINO RITZ TO THE RESCUE

Looked like a *monster*.

—He's not small. Denis put in. —Must be at least seven feet tall. We thought it best to retreat and reconnoiter some more.

—At the Wax Museum. Ernest stared off over the rooftops of North Beach at the Eiffel Tower. —I wonder what is going on. But you didn't see Sherwood?

—No, we didn't. There was this big black box-like thing and this huge guy guarding it. We were both a little loaded, you know, enough to be a little unsteady on our feet, so we scouted around but we couldn't find any way to get back there. It looked like you'd have to open one of the exhibits and get back there that way.

—And that's all the plaque said: *Sherwood Anderson,* and his dates, in little white letters that glowed in the dark.

—Yeah.

Ernest stood up and grinned. —Well boys, it looks like we're going to have to make a little assault on a Wax Museum tonight.

The attack was to be two-pronged: Alice and Gertrude were to provide the diversion for the guards of the Wax Museum out front, while F. Scott and Denis and Ernest swept in through the back door of the warehouse behind the Wax Museum.

Denis had outfitted himself with a shillelagh. Ernest had armed himself with one of his Duo-Flex X-17 spear guns. F. Scott had come equipped with a handful of pointy swizzle sticks and a rather long and impressive plasticized railway-share which he claimed acted like a boomerang.

—Lost my ass on this one back in '29—but I liked its engraving so much I had it plasticized. . . .

The plan called for Alice to set up a portable cookstove in front of the Wax Museum, and for Gertrude to play the mandolin and sing, just as if they were street musicians trying to make a buck or two.

While they diverted attention outside, the three in back would break into the warehouse and see what was up with the big black box with Sherwood's name on it.

The first part of the plan went off quite well. Alice and Gertrude were singing and cooking out front, attracting a great deal of attention as the break-in began in back.

Actually there was no need for the complex set of keys that Ernest had obtained for the type of lock on the door. Someone had forgotten to lock it, so the three were in much sooner than anticipated.

This easy entry upset Denis, although he denied it later. He was extremely apprehensive as they entered: so apprehensive as to imagine someone in the dark behind the door. He suspected a trap, although he denied this later, too.

Exactly what happened after Denis lunged with his shillelagh at the person behind the door was hard for the participants to come to any agreement on. . . .

Unfortunately the door opened just to the left of the big black box where Sherwood was imprisoned, so the first thing Ernest saw, once his eyes became used to the dark, was the rather imposing figure of Abraham Lincoln in front of the box.

Ernest had raised his spear gun to cover the giant when Denis lunged into the shadows after the imaginary person there and accidently hit the control panel for the Abraham Lincoln robot.

F. Scott, who was between Ernest and Denis, swore that he heard the noise of a huge crowd, when actually the sound of the Abraham Lincoln robot was all he heard. The tape had been shut off right after Abe said

HOWDY ILLINOIS

in German, and the next statement was in Japanese.

The combination of the giant Abraham Lincoln raising his arm in a fascist salute and saying

HOWDY ILLINOIS

in Japanese, at an extremely high amplification (Denis' shillelagh must have upped the volume as it raked the control panel), caused Ernest to panic, briefly, and he fired his spear gun.

Meanwhile, out in the front of the Wax Museum, Alice and Gertrude had just been called over by the ticket taker, and asked to move on. Alice was holding a pan of bechamel sauce up on the counter of the ticket window when the spear pierced the giant Abraham Lincoln inside and short-circuited all the lights of the Wax Museum.

The lights blowing out so frightened Alice that she spilled the bechamel sauce all over Mr. Ching's ticket counter, and all over Mr. Ching.

The combination of the lights blowing out and the hot bechamel sauce on his hands and lap caused Mr. Ching to a-bandon the scientific rationality which had won him his Docter of Science degree. He rushed out of the booth and attacked Alice, thinking the sauce had caused the short-circuit.

Unfortunately for Mr. Ching, Gertrude was behind him with her mandolin held high.

Simultaneous with the braining of Dr. Ching, all three of the intruders in back were struggling with the door, which had locked behind them after they slipped in. The giant Abraham Lincoln was doing a herky-jerky series of straight-armed salutes as his circuits exploded inside him.

When the walls of the cage cleared an hour later, Sherwood Anderson found himself looking down at a group of solemn-looking Japanese, all standing in a circle around the giant Abraham Lincoln. A long spear was sticking through the Abe's side, and a plasticized railway-share was lodged in his neck.

One of the Japanese was holding a handful of plastic swizzle sticks in his hand, and looking down at them with a puzzled expression..

Later, they argued about why it couldn't have been done another way. —There was no need to brain that ticket-taker with your mandolin, F. Scott had said to Gertrude.

—He was about to assault Alice.

—Wouldn't you be upset if someone spilled a pan full of bechamel sauce all over your ticket counter and across your lap? Can you imagine cleaning that out of those little slots and in between the keys?

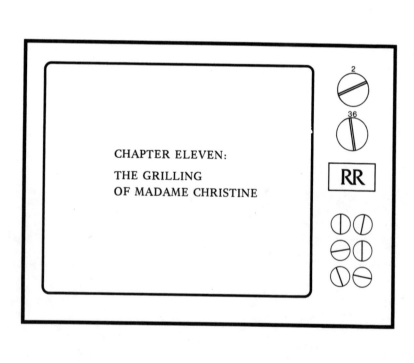

CHAPTER ELEVEN:

THE GRILLING
OF MADAME CHRISTINE

One thing about Smitty: as an operative for Rhino Ritz, no one could beat him. He melded into a crowd like a hot BB dropped in butter.

Michael Soul left the Yoshimura Camera Company and went straight over to Paris, pausing only at a small smut store on Market Street. He was carrying a large, fat briefcase when he went in and when he came out, he had a bundle under his arm, wrapped in brown paper.

When he entered Paris, he went straight to the Gare St. Lazare and stood around by the ticket windows for a while, as if he were waiting for someone.

Smitty had donned a delivery man's uniform, with a white shirt and tie under it, in case he had to look formal. He also had a beret in his back pocket which he could switch with the delivery man's hat.

At what seemed like a perfectly random moment, Soul left the ticket windows, went down to the trains, and took the Sunset District express.

Smitty couldn't see anyone with him, although it was hard to be sure, as he had to stay one car back and watch him through the window in the sliding door between cars.

He got out on Taraval and continued down the street toward the ocean. Just as Smitty turned the corner, he saw Soul slip into a bright red Tornado parked at the curb. The car slowly pulled out and drove off toward Daly City.

Smitty kept it in sight as long as he could, then ran back up to 19th Avenue and flagged down a cab. It was pretty hopeless, but he went back down to where he'd last seen the red car and began to circle the blocks.

He didn't have any luck until he reached the Zoo:

the Tornado was parked in front of the Ocean Park Motel.

—Pardon me, Smitty said to the clerk, a fat woman with a face as pocked and florid as a diseased batch of Kandy Korn, —a friend of mine said he might be checking in out here: a Mr. . . .

Luckily there was no alias. Smitty declined the offer of a phone call and acted as if Mr. Soul were expecting him. He walked around the court until he found Room 117. It was out of the clerk's sight so he didn't bother to knock, but instead peeked in through a gap in the drapes.

From his point of view, he had never seen anything like it before.

Madame Christine was on the bed, tied up with ropes. Michael Soul seemed to be somewhere to the right, where Smitty couldn't see him. Madame Christine had a calm, almost detached look. Her eyes blinked a couple of times. Then she was entirely consumed by a flickering blue light.

Across the flat, body-shaped blue light there ap-peared a writhing of organic black lines. A milky white wave kept rolling up through the blue light.

Just then Michael Soul stepped into Smitty's field of vision. Smitty instinctively stepped back from the window. He looked up and down the courtyard: only a few honeybees circling under the hibiscus beside one of the doors. All the curtains were closed in the rooms on the opposite row.

Smitty put his face back to the glass.

Soul was now wearing a tight black leather thong that wrapped around his thighs in a curious cross-hatched pattern which left his genitals free.

The swirling black and white lines on the blue surface of Madame Christine were now particularized and focused enough so that Smitty could see two bodies forming in the blue projected light.

It looked like a film of a man and a woman making love.

Smitty looked nervously around the courtyard again. It was hot. He felt himself sweating. Still the drowsy afternoon sun on the gravel, the brick borders, the orange flowers hanging down, limp.

When he looked back again, he could see that Soul had entered the blue projection and was. . . .

Smitty didn't know how to see what he was seeing.

It looked like Michael Soul was entering the images on top
of Madame Christine's body while she was pulling him
through from the other side.

Actually what it looked like was a man and a woman
both making love to a blue cloud. Smitty wondered what
things looked like on the other side of the image . . . what
it must look like to her . . . and to. . . .

Smitty came to. And found himself standing by the
entrance to the motel. He realized, slowly, that he'd wan-
dered away after being sucked into a cloud of speculative
androgeny. He shook his head and took a deep breath.

Now he'd been in the Navy, Smitty had, and he'd
been to some pretty strange events in the brothels of Bang-
kok. But he'd never been even remotely as launched off the
pad with mental sex as he had just been with *that* little
show.

He got in the cab. The cabbie looked over his shoulder at him without bothering to put down the *Chronicle.*

—You find your friends? he asked.

—Go around the corner and park down about two
blocks. When that red Tornado leaves, follow it.

The cabbie eyed Smitty for a moment, almost said
something, then started the cab. —Hot out there, ain't it?
You look a little white.

Smitty was adjusting his camera in the back seat and
didn't say anything. He wondered why he hadn't taken any
pictures. He found that he was having trouble with the lens;
then he saw that his hands were trembling.

*Lucky I didn't try to take any pictures,* he thought,

*I probably would have shoved the lens right through the window.*

—Preeeeeety Kink-EEE! was all F. Scott could say, grinning.

Ernest and Gertrude and Alice were considerably less amused. —You're *sure* it was Madame Christine, then?

—Yeah, from the description we got from Mlle. Love over there at Sherwood's hotel, I would say it was. Plus, well, I mean she was doing those things just. . . .

—So there's a second connection now between Sherwood and the Camera Corporation, Gertrude cut in. She did not want the conversation to become *inaccrochable.*

—Possibly. I got a few quick pictures of Soul leaving the motel. All we have to do is show them to Mlle. Love and see if he's the guy who rented the room next to Sherwood's.

—What were they doing again? F. Scott said, glancing over at the prim threesome of Ernest, Gertrude and Alice. —They were using the P.O.V. machine?

—Well, she was tied up and he seemed to be projecting a bunch of porno flicks onto her aura, and then, you know, uh, entering her through the uh, images. . . .

—Where's Denis? Gertrude cut in.

—Both men and women? F. Scott persisted.

Smitty shrugged and looked to the heavens. —Whatever gets you through the night, I guess. All they are are images. Sort of like you guys, actually. Not much difference between a myth and an image, not in this day and age. Used to be one was bigger and fuller than the other but now. . . .

—Maybe it's some sort of therapy, Alice said sweetly.

—Therapy, shit! Ernest said. —Look, let's not dwell on these matters. They're of no importance to finding out where they're holding Sherwood.

—Well, we don't know if they are holding Sherwood at the Wax Museum or not, since you three botched it.

—We *didn't* botch it!

—A fire engine and four police cars and alarms and a crowd just slightly under a thousand people is a successful covert operation?

—*Now Lovey,* Alice put in, placing her hand on Gertrude's arm.

—Well, at least they don't know what happened.

—But even the newspapers didn't say Sherwood Anderson was locked up in that cube, or box, or whatever it was.

—Why would they look?

The phone rang.

Ernest answered, and after a minute turned back to the group. —Denis says there's a guard on the door now, and no one is going in or out. He says he wants to be relieved too. Scott?

—Why do *I* have to go?

—We can't exactly have Gertrude or Alice hanging around there, now can we? I mean, after they brained that ticket-taker, he's sure to recognize them and just *might* call the police.

—We can go with you and talk to Madame Christine, can't we?

But Alice and Gertrude didn't come along after all, as they had to return to their penance at Fort Point. Which was fortunate, considering how things turned out.

Ernest and Smitty decided to drive over to 243 Collins St. where Madame Christine was staying, above a used TV and TV repair shop. Ernest was so grumpy enough about the assault of the night before that he needed to get a little air. So Smitty strapped him on the back of the flatbed and he braved the cool San Francisco fog that shredded around his speeding hulk like "a rotting shroud" (or so he put it to himself as he watched it happen).

On Masonic Smitty unstrapped him and they walked around to Collins St. Smitty went to a phone booth out on Geary Boulevard and made a call. —She's there, he said.

After killing time for about a half an hour they went up to the upstairs apartment. A gutted Zenith TV set sat in the doorway of the TV repair shop. Smitty looked at it and wondered how many of those were taking up space in the world. This particular model looked like a cheap pine casket for the world's largest glass eye.

Madame Christine answered the door in her negligee. She didn't seem surprised to see a man in a huge cardboard box next to a short dude standing like dummies in her doorway. She'd been around.

—What is it? she asked. She seemed *very* impatient.

Later that afternoon Ernest and Smitty returned to the Rhino Ritz office on Union Street. Ernest immediately went to the front room and began typing his report. Smitty retired with Denis to the kitchen. The report was as follows:

We arrived at the informant's flat at 243 Collins shortly after the noon hour. The fog was just beginning to clear from the tops of the houses around Masonic. Informant was still in her dressing gown. She invited us in and led us up the stairs.

The flat was painted white. It was clean and looked relatively unused.

"You just move in?" I said.

"Yes," she said, "but I hardly own anything anyway."

We sat down at a long polished oak table and she got the coffee from the kitchen. Through the window behind her head the mist was parting. The tops of the houses and the billboards were beginning to glimmer in the sun.

"We know about Soul," I said.

"So?"

"Why did you do it?"

"That's my business. What's yours?"

"Look, things can be easy or things can be hard."

"Either way's fine with me."

"What about Sherwood."

"What about who?"

"We know you were seeing Sherwood Anderson, and we know you were staying out with him nights, and we know that you were softening him up for something."

"That's *not* what I usually do."

I got up and walked over to the window as she shifted around on the chaise lounge. She looked up at me and began to smile, but I caught her hand and bent the little finger over into her palm. Hard.

"Jesus Christ!"

"Tell me about Sherwood and why Soul put you up to it and what he wanted out of it."

"Jesus Christ, you don't have to do *that*."

"Let her go," Smitty said, "she'll talk."

"Jesus Christ," she said, looking at her finger.

"We're waiting."

She stretched her finger out a little. Then she looked up at me. Then she looked over at Smitty. She shrugged.

"It was just a job."

"You mean he hired you to take up with Sherwood," I said.

"What was your cover?" Smitty asked.

"I was supposed to play a Midwestern girl. Not hard, considering I come from Michigan."

"So?"

"So I talked to him and we had a few nights together and then we got to *reminiscing* and I swear to God he liked that better than sex and we'd sing those songs, and they were okay but not that okay, and then I got a call and dropped him."

"From Soul?"

"Yeah, from Soul."

"So why'd you move?"

"He said I should, and set me up here for two months worth of rent."

"Plus payment for the Sherwood caper?" Smitty asked.

"Yeah."

"What about your motel visits?"

Madame Christine glanced over at Smitty and then looked back at the doorway to the kitchen. "If you know so much, why. . . ."

"Should we bother with her any more?" I asked Smitty.

"No, I don't see why."

"You guys aren't going to get rough, are you?"

"I don't think we should bother with this anymore," I said, taking her by the arm and lifting her off the couch.

She started to talk and she didn't stop until we told her to.

—Ya ever try to give the third degree to an S&M master call-girl? Smitty asked Denis plaintively. —Jesus, she kept interrupting us with hints.

—Really? Denis said, taking a deep sniff of the wine and holding it up to the light. Duo-Flex X-17 Merlot, 1971.

—Well, Smitty said as he looked around and saw that Ernie had stopped typing in the other room and was making a phone call, —don't tell nobody, but it just didn't work out like we wanted. I mean, I thought we had it knocked. Rough her up a little if she don't want to talk and then split with the news. . . . No way.

Smitty stopped and looked in at Ernie. —Don't say I told you, he said, nodding toward the other room, —but it worked out real A-okay anyway.

Denis eyed Smitty. —You mean, you gentlemen took advantage of the poor girl?

—Yeah well . . . she took us both on. What the hell, Smitty said, shrugging. —I mean, she was holding out and we were doing all the right stuff, slapping cigarettes out of her hand and playing kinda rough and she was acting so innocent and all . . . I mean, we forgot who we were dealing with.

Denis smiled with anticipated vicarious appreciation. —And so then?

Smitty looked in again at Ernie's room and began talking even lower. —Well, we had her tied up in a chair and we were threatening her.

—Go on, my son.

—And she said she was gonna pass out and she'd tell us if we loosened the rope . . . I mean, we were so far into

this, you know how Ernie is, he even brought a blackjack,
and she started squirming and fighting once we did that, and
managed to fall out of the chair and work loose—I don't
know how she did that—and we threw her down on the bed
and looped one rope around the bedpost and that's when
she began to tell us what to do. It was crazy, and jesus, she
got ahold of me too, don't ask me how, and the next thing
I knew she was working on me, insteada, well. . . .

Smitty sighed. —Then you know what happened? She
gets up and starts talking to us just as if nothing happened
at all. She goes out and makes some coffee, one rope drag-
ging after her, just like nothing happened at all. Chirpy as a
goddamn sparrow. *"All in a day's work, all in a day's work,"*
she kept saying. Of course then we had to give her some
money, but shit, that was easier than trying to wrestle it out
of her. We were laying there on the bed bushed, I don't
know why we didn't offer it to her in the first place. . . .

Denis nodded sagely. —Yes, lucky Gertrude and Alice
weren't along. They weren't likely to join in.

—Yeah, but it sure was weird, I mean, under the boss's
*box.* . . .

Ernest came into the hallway, stopped for a moment as
if thinking, then continued into the kitchen. Smitty stopped
talking to Denis.

—So what's the scoop? he said to Ernest.

—Soul's in his office and I hung up on the secretary.
We'll go down and throw it right up in his puss. He'll spill.
Ernest shrugged his box. —Just like she did.

CHAPTER TWELVE:

THE WRITERS' MARKET

—Now what did she say?

—Didn't you read my report?

—Yes, Ernest, I read your report. You better not let it slip out to anyone else.

—I know, I know.

—Not that *they're* going to find out what she said from it either.

—What do you mean? Ernest stopped watching the mime at Washington Square and turned back to look at Gertrude on the other side of the limousine.

—You forget sometimes, Ernest, to leave in the parts that tell a person something. However, it was a nice mood. Now what did she say?

Ernest glanced over at Gertrude and then looked at Alice between them, but she was watching the mime. —She said that she was paid to talk to Sherwood and make him homesick for Ohio. That's all she knows. She said they had a little, uh, . . . well, affair, and then she said they just got together and drank and sang old cowboy songs and old hillbilly songs. But she was paid by this guy Soul who then told her to move out of Paris into the Richmond district. Even paid two months rent on the place. She said sure. She didn't care where she lived. She could stand to stay out of Paris. Too much competition down there anyway.

—What did she seem to think it was all about?

—She didn't know.

—Was she being truthful?

—Well, I don't know. We had to play a little rough with her there for a. . . .

—I wish you could have brought us along, Hemingway.

We could have told you whether or not she was lying. You're not exactly the most perceptive observer of the female species, you know. . . .

F. Scott turned around from the front seat. —Yeah, I thought you'd have her saying *"Yes darling,"* over and over again by the end of the report.

Ernest's face reddened and he looked from Gertrude to F. Scott and back again. But he didn't say anything.

—She wasn't hurt, was she? Alice put in.

—Naw, she wasn't *hurt.* But she didn't know any more than that. Said the guy Soul did get. . . . I mean, later he saw her but that was . . . just more business. Ernest looked uncomfortable. —Why don't you lay off me. I'm tired.

—What about the P.O.V. machine?

—She brought that up herself, Smitty said from the front seat.

Ernest looked at the back of his head severely. —He means she told us about it. She didn't have one. She said it left her, well, she felt almost sucked dry by the damn thing. Made her thirsty. Ernest hesitated.

—She said he . . . liked it that way. He shrugged. —Not that it bothers *me.*

—Didn't bother *her* either, Smitty murmured from the front.

F. Scott began to discuss slang with the black limo driver. The rest of them fell silent.

—Is that the term for that now? We used to say we were going to conk him, or they were going to conk him for sure. That was it, *conk him for sure.*

–That used to be a hair style awhile back. I don't know if they still call it that. But it was a hair style, not a killing, the driver said.

Michael Soul was a dapper little man. He sat behind his dark
stained desk with the grace of a grasshopper. His hands
moved this way and that: sure, complete. He looked up and
smiled at them as the last soft shuffle of paper dissolved in
the cool air of his office.

—Now that's done, we can talk. I'm afraid you are
right, but there is nothing even remotely illegal about the entire operation, so your fears are exaggerated and this in turn
has colored your point of view on the matter.

Ernest stared at Soul's gray suit and bright silk *rep* tie
and noted the way he tugged gently at the soft blue french
cuffs of his sleeves as he walked over to the huge window
overlooking the tideflats. Beyond the rusted girders and the
warehouses, a black and white freighter flying a Japanese
flag slowly steamed toward the Golden Gate Bridge.

—Nothing in the remotest sense illegal about it. The
same as an advertising campaign, exactly the same. Only
each one was directed at one individual.

Ernest looked at Gertrude. She seemed calm, non-com-
mital. F. Scott looked bothered, almost stymied, as if he
were incapable of soaking this up the way he soaked up so
much of the rest of the world.

But it was all clear to Gertrude, so she continued the
questioning.

—Well, she said, —tell us how you did it.

Michael Soul flicked his eyes over Gertrude and then
smiled, as if acknowledging her neutral tone as correct. Or
perhaps just what he expected. He pressed a button on the
mini-switchboard inset in his desk.

A Japanese girl in a short red dress with a small blue

scarf about her neck wheeled in a brown suitcase mounted on a cart. She dismantled the suitcase and revealed a very small projector.

—Would you like to be the screen, Mr. Hemingway?

—No, Ernest said, —I wouldn't. I understand it really takes it out of you.

Michael Soul didn't show any reaction at all to the comment. He merely nodded at the girl and she switched on the P.O.V. machine.

It was aimed at a huge rubber plant. This plant was instantly transformed into a pond with a green pasture beyond it, dotted with grazing cattle and one huge oak tree. The deep blue Midwestern sky above it. . . .

—Sherwood was the easiest of all of you. Of course the machine functioned perfectly. But then you probably already know that. We knew we'd have quite a time convincing you other four.

He shrugged. —Such is the nature of artistic perversity.

Ernest grunted. —Talk about perversity, he began to say.

Michael Soul ignored him and he fell silent. —Now what is unique about this is the way in which it is real. And it *is* real. As real as you want it to be. Naturally someone like Sherwood has a great deal of faith to invest in such things as this: Ohio, Iowa, whatever you want to call it. . . .

—But he did sign a *contract?*

—Why of course! I wouldn't lie to you. Otherwise it would be kidnapping.

—Like those guys who got Alice and Gertrude?

Michael Soul looked perturbed. —That was so . . . unnecessary. Unfortunate. Believe me, we had nothing to do with that.

—Then this check here is just a coincidence.

Michael Soul made no move toward the check in Ernest's hand. —Of course. We heard about it over the TV the same as you did. Our scout brought it to our attention and I thought it an excellent opportunity to show our good will and concern, as I instructed our. . . .

—Tattered karate chop, F. Scott put in.

—What?

—Nothing.

—So I instructed our lawyers to negotiate any release payment. As a gesture of our goodwill. . . .

—Shit, Ernest snorted.

Gertrude glanced once at Ernest and then said: —So you have Sherwood now, and he's on his way.

—Yes, he looked at his watch, —he should be loaded by now. Perhaps not. He grimaced. —These workers . . . of yours are so dreadfully . . . inefficient. Slow.

—So you think he's going to be a big draw over there?

—Why yes. The Japanese people have a great interest in your writing. He will be much better taken care of there than he is in that dingy Parisian dive. . . .

Michael Soul went over to the window and pulled the curtain back, revealing the Eiffel Tower and North Beach beyond it. —That's where you live, isn't it?

Ernest didn't answer him. He only stared at Coit Tower for a moment and then looked away.

—Must be rather drafty.

—Then these little visions we've been having have all
been part of this . . . what did you call it?

—Well, in the trade it's known as a Single Objective Ad
Campaign. We sell a buyer or customer subliminally before
he knows he's being. . . .

—Bought or sold, F. Scott put in.

—No, convinced. Convinced is the correct word.

—But there's a bit more to it than that, isn't there?

—What do you mean? he said, turning to Ernest.

—Creating a market for the other product, the alabaster
diamond over there in Iowa, that's what I mean. Subsidizing
the other product at the expense of ours.

Michael Soul shrugged. —Universities are slow markets
but they're coming along. They have their uses. The market
is going that way anyway, and they tag along. We're just giving them a boost. No different than a chemical company giving them money for their chemistry department scholarships.

—We just helped the market along. Interest in you here
is going down, has been for years. So why not?

—I mean, you have to make an effort to understand
our point of view on the matter. You like approbation, we
like money.

The four of them were silent.

—You may be immortal but what is that? Nothing. I
mean really.

F. Scott shrugged. —I don't know what good it will do
you. We can't write, not that I'd want to anyway. Our
contract.

—So much the better. Immortal writers are so much
easier to manage that way than live ones. That way *we* get

to produce the books. And most of what has come after you are just P.O.V. machines in wrappers anyway. What with the current psychic strip-mining scene, we can get people to buy back their own minds four or more times a year as it is . . . each time with brand new terms and up-to-date fantasies.

 —Look, we really have your interest at heart with this offer. We want to remove you from . . . and take you where you're appreciated.

 He walked over to a door behind them.

 —Now here's our sales rep for Writerland. Lovely location, just outside of Kyoto. He wants to distribute the details of our amusement park and cultural zoo and tell you what you can expect if you join us. I realized that we were taking a big chance with your Single Objective Ad Campaign but then again, you can see that this is a creative company.

 —Sterling, would you like to come in and explain to the ladies and gentlemen the terms of our agreement?

 —Sterling Phillips, Yoshimura's main man in charge of cultural illusions. He'll show you what you have to gain. . . . Sterling, meet our authors.

There were four longshoremen adjusting the net around Sherwood's black box when they arrived at the wharf. The winch strained and the men stepped back. Slowly the net went taut and the grind and whine of the crane's boom and cable filled the air. The seagulls sat silent on the roof of the neighboring pier as Sherwood was winched up onto the deck of the Japanese freighter.

F. Scott and Ernest stood in the open doors of the limo. A glossy brochure hanging out of F. Scott's coat pocket flapped in the breeze.

Denis sidled up to Ernest and tapped him on his box.
—Where you guys been? I've been trying to get ahold of you all afternoon. They moved the box out this morning.

—He was in there, Ernest said, —all the time he was in there.

Back at Rhino Ritz's office, F. Scott leafed slowly through the Yoshimura pamphlet. At his feet lay the glossy brochure describing the park. Ernest was pacing around the room. Gertrude and Alice were sitting on the couch in the corner.

—Dying was bad enough but being bought and sold too. . . . I thought I left all that shit behind me when we went immortal. But . . . perhaps there will be a revival. . . .

No one said anything.

—I don't know how. We're played out as people. . . . You know what they're going to do, they're going to get as many of us over there as possible and then . . . then they're going to sell us back to . . . sell us back here.

—Well, Ernest, that wasn't exactly what happened to us before, you know, but it did help that we were in Paris and Paris was all the rage then, you know. . . .

—But this is different, Scott. That wasn't just us, that was a whole . . . it was bigger than just us. This is so . . . goddamn personally manipulative. . . .

—You heard the man: single ad objective. The Mind's the place where it's bought and sold, and *what* is bought and sold.

—Maybe they'll let us write over there, Gertrude said.

—Now don't you start that, Ernest said, swinging around to face Gertrude. —It'll be no different over there about *that.*

Later that night on the Rue Christine, Gertrude was sitting on the bed as Alice undressed. She was staring at the pamphlet in her hand. Slowly she brought the glossy brochure out from under it and stared at it for a time. Alice sat down beside her. She was wearing a silk negligee that contrasted oddly with Gertrude's rough red flannel nightgown. She put her chin on Gertrude's shoulder and her hand just where Gertrude's arm lay lightly on her leg.

In the color photograph of Stein's front room there was a bookcase lined with orange-backed leather books. In the light from the fireplace the gold lettering gleamed.

—I don't know, Pussy.

Alice looked up at Gertrude's face, soft and full in the lamp's light.

—Maybe it wouldn't be so bad to be sold back to America.